Vent's face suddenly turned bleak and cold as he looked at Bright. "Take your hand off that gun, you son of a bitch, or you're dead meat."

Bright jerked his hand away from his pistol and, looking at Stalls, asked plaintively, "You gonna let him get away with calling me that?"

Stalls stared at him. "Dammit, Bobby, that's between you and him."

Bright stood mute.

Ignoring him then, Vent looked at Stalls and said quietly, "Mr. Stalls, you're wasting your time. I ain't going anywhere with you. You go back and tell Elam Jordan if he wants to talk to me, why he can just straddle a horse and name the neutral ground and I'll be there."

Stalls shook his head stubbornly. "That ain't my orders, Mr. Torrey."

Vent's eyes narrowed. "You ready to die for your orders?"

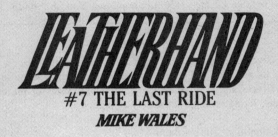

LEATHERHAND

#7 THE LAST RIDE

MIKE WALES

PINNACLE BOOKS   NEW YORK

This novel is a work of fiction. Names, characters, places, and incidents are either the product of the author's imagination or are used fictitiously. Any resemblance to actual events or places or persons, living or dead, is entirely coincidental.

LEATHERHAND #7: THE LAST RIDE

Copyright © 1985 by Mike Wales

An original Pinnacle Books edition, published for the first time anywhere.

First printing/May 1985

ISBN: 0-523-42318-7
Can. ISBN: 0-523-43326-3

Printed in the United States of America

PINNACLE BOOKS, INC.
1430 Broadway
New York, New York 10018

9 8 7 6 5 4 3 2 1

This book is dedicated to James H. Martin, who put me on my first bronc and watched me buck off

THE LAST RIDE

Chapter One

The tall, broad-shouldered man in the gray hat and the heavy batwing chaps rode down the main street of South Pass City, his eyes automatically checking both street and sidewalk traffic. Men who noticed him usually took a second look. He was a man to remember as he sat solidly in the seat of the Texas centerfire saddle on the back of the powerful Appaloosa. The horse appeared as alert as its master, for it moved along the street with head up and ears forward.

There was a slight bite to the air and the man on the Appaloosa rode with his left hand in the pocket of a black-and-white mackinaw while the right hand gripped the reins. It was this hand that caught the attention of several sidewalk loungers. It was covered by a heavy leather glove, interlaced with straps that held it in place and reinforced the back of the hand and wrist of the man who wore it. He rode with reins low, leaving the oddly gloved hand within easy reach of the heavy .44 Colt pistol riding on his right hip, its wooden grips showing years of hard usage. Beneath his right leg a scabbard held a 38.40

1

Winchester rifle, its brass frame polished to a reflective brightness by the leather of its long gun holster.

Spring was just finding its way to this mile-high city perched on the eastern slope of the Great Divide, a few short miles from the Continental Divide. It was on a direct route to California and had seen its share of immigrants on their way to Oregon and points west. It also had been, and still was, home to a number of men who made their living off other men's cattle, over the card tables, or over a blazing gun.

Isom Dart, the black rustler and gunman, made his home here when not riding in and out of Brown's Hole with the Wild Bunch. Jesse Ewing and Tom Horn had both frequented this mean scrabble of shacks on the high plains of Wyoming and had left their mark in Boot Hill, where the earthly remains of men who were fool enough to test their legends were interred.

The man on the Appaloosa swung the animal over to stop at a water trough and wait patiently while the horse drank its fill, then, as it lifted its head and rattled the bit chains, a man stopped on the sidewalk, turned on his heel, and walked to the opposite side of the trough and had his look at horse and man, then asked, "You wanta sell that animal?"

The rider laid his full gaze on the speaker and when the man met his eyes, he suddenly shook his head and said, "No, I don't reckon you would," and walked away.

The rider of the Appaloosa smiled and turning the horse, rode along the street until he reached a combination saloon and eating place and, rounding into the hitchrack, stepped down, unloosened the cinch and, tossing the reins over the rack, stepped up on the sidewalk, glanced both ways, then entered the building. As he passed from the brightness of day into the semi-gloom of the long bar, he stepped to the right and placed his back against the wall, waited a short moment for his eyes to adjust to the light, then had his look at the patrons and noted they were the usual polyglot of drifters, saloon hangers-on, gamblers, pimps, touts, and flash gunmen. There were several dancehall girls the tall man knew charged a quarter for a round on the floor and a dollar for a round upstairs.

Noting an empty table near the end of the room, the man made his way to it and sat with his back to the wall, folded his hands on top of the table, and waited patiently for someone to come and take his order. While he waited, he carefully examined each face along the bar and then inventoried the card tables.

"What'll it be, friend?" a waiter inquired, and the young man in the gray hat looked up at him and asked, "You got beef?"

"Yes sir . . . with potatoes, biscuits, and good gravy, along with coffee that'll melt a six-shooter."

The traveler smiled and said, "Bring me a full order and while I'm waiting for it, fetch me two glasses of your best whiskey," and watched the waiter move away.

When the whiskey arrived, he drank the first shot with a quick flip of his wrist and left the other sitting.

Several men and at least three of the women in the place had noticed him and were looking his way curiously. The appearance of a stranger in South Pass City was not unusual, for the town lay on a well-traveled route, but the man in the gray hat had a different look about him. He seemed surrounded by an aura of quiet calmness that defied penetration. Anyone looking at him would have guessed that whatever he did to earn his daily bread was done efficiently and with little fanfare or effort.

The gloved hand had also attracted some glances. One of the lookers, a diminutive blonde with large blue eyes and breasts so large as to make her appear top-heavy, decided to get acquainted. She strolled over to the traveler's table and leaning down, asked, "You want some company, mister?"

Raising his head, he stared into her eyes and suddenly she lost her ability to speak. The brown eyes seemed to have no bottoms and something cold and deadly moved in their depths; something that turned the girl away from the table with a shrug. She did not look back as she walked to the bar and ordered a whiskey and lifted it with a hand that shook as she drank it down.

The bartender, a man who had spent the spring and summer of his life in some hard places, and was now coming up on the last lap of his allotted time, had seen his share of bad men and, after watching the girl and her reaction to the man with the odd leather glove, looked toward the shotgun guard who sat on his perch overlooking the card tables, a sawed-down, double-barreled ten-gauge across his lap, and slowly nodded his head.

The guard, who had also seen the girl's reaction, shifted his position slightly, bringing the barrel of the deadly Greener around to a position that would only require seconds to spin it and fire.

None of this passed the observation of the traveler. He had seen the same thing happen in a hundred such places. Hard men recognized their own kind and until they knew the aims and temperament of the other fellow, they did not take chances. The man who shot first lived to brag about it to the saloon girls. The man who shot last was forgotten half an hour after the Mexican gravedigger tramped down the last shovel full of dirt.

The waiter crossed the room with the traveler's meal and just before he reached the table, a boot was thrust out and the man, tripping over it, pitched forward, hurling the tray and its burden onto the floor to mix with the sawdust, spittle, and spilled drinks.

Grinning broadly, the man who had tripped the waiter turned to his companions and said loudly, "Did you fellers see that? Why old Jake's sure gettin' clumsy. Fell right smack dab over my boot," and then he looked boldly at the traveler and the grin turned impudent.

The traveler rose and shrugging, picked up his second whiskey, drank it away, and walked past the offender's table. As he stepped around its grinning drinkers, he suddenly stopped and whipped out the heavy .44 in a move so swift men who witnessed it were later to proclaim they never even saw the draw. With a vicious backhand swipe, he slammed the barrel and cylinder into the offender's mouth, cracking several of his teeth and knocking him unconscious on the floor.

In almost the same instant, one of the other men at the table, a slim, over-dressed kid wearing two guns, drew one of them only to find it pinned to the table. The traveler had driven a long, thin dagger through the back of his hand. Screaming, he tried to jerk the hand free, but only succeeded in cutting it worse.

When the stranger went into action, the shotgunner began his swiveling movement, but before he could bring his deadly weapon to bare, he was looking down the bore of the .44 as the man behind it said in the sudden stillness, "I wouldn't try it on if I was you, friend."

The man with his hand pinned began to whimper, then said in anguish, "Oh, God, he's ruined my gunhand . . . Oooooo . . ."

At that moment the front door swung open and a broad-shouldered man wearing a handlebar mustache and his hair to his shoulders stepped into the room, took in the scene and said softly, "Now what have we got going here?"

No one spoke.

Being careful with his hands, the newcomer pulled his coat to one side, exposing a marshal's badge, and extracted a cigar from a shirt pocket. Biting off the end, he thrust it between his teeth and removing a match from his hat band, lit it, blew smoke at the ceiling and said casually, "Howdy, Vent. How are ya?"

Vent Torrey, the man known all over the west as Leatherhand, did not take his eyes off the shotgunner, but instead, said, "Hep, reckon you best tell that jigger with the crowd killer I'm going to wait another half minute for him to drop that thing and if he don't, I'm going to kill him."

Glancing at the guard, the marshal grinned and said, "Bill Smaldeen, meet Vent Torrey. . . . They sometimes call him Leatherhand. . . ."

Every man in the saloon had heard of the man with the leather glove on his hand. Like the tigerskin chaps worn by the gunfighter, King Fisher, the gloved hand had become a symbol of another kind of gunfighter. Vent Torrey did not sell his gun, unless one could call marshaling a gun job. Unlike Fisher, the man called Leatherhand only used his gun when necessity demanded it. Now he waited to see what the guard would do.

He didn't have long to wait. The man very carefully placed the weapon on the floor at his feet and straightening up, put both hands on the rail in front of him.

Vent nodded and then looked down as the man he had pistolwhipped rolled over and sat up. Shaking his head, he spit out two teeth and a mouthful of blood and then, suddenly remembering what had happened to him, clawed for his gun.

Vent kicked him in the wrist and the breaking of the bone was loud in that silent room. Clutching his injured member, the man looked up and said bitterly, "You better kill me 'cause if you don't, you're a dead man."

"Suit yourself," Vent replied and, dropping the pistol against the side of the man's head, started to take up the slack in the trigger when he shouted, "No, no . . . wait . . . don't . . . don't do that . . ."

Lifting the pistol, Vent shrugged and said, "Make up your mind."

"Mind if I come on in?" Hep Alkire asked.

"Come ahead," Vent nodded and the marshal walked to the bar and glancing at the bartender, asked, "What started this here shindig?"

"Tag Bitters there, he thought it might be downright funny if he just up and tripped old Jake. So happens Jake was toting a tray with Mr. Torrey's food on it . . . Reckon maybe Mr. Torrey was some hungry to get that mad . . ."

Glancing at Jake, Vent said, "Put in another order, mister, and if anybody tries to trip you this time, I'm going to blow his damn kneecap off," and Vent turned his head in a sweep of the bar. Nobody met his gaze. Stepping around behind the kid with the flashy clothes, he reached over and grasped the handle of his knife and jerked it loose from the table and the boy's hand. As it came free, the kid screamed and passed out, sliding to the floor.

Looking down at him, Vent said, "Somebody oughta tell this pup it doesn't take a man to wear a gun, but it damned sure takes one to know when to use it."

The marshal strolled over and looked at the kid, then relieved him of his second gun and picked up the one he had tried to use on Vent and, walking to the bar, tossed them to the bartender and ordered, "Stash these things, Curly, and don't give them back to that kid until he sees me," and he walked back and looked down at the bloodied Tag Bitters and said coldly, "Tag, you just seem to love to start trouble. I'm putting you on notice. You come to my town again and stir up a ruckus and I'll kill you out of hand. You hear me?''

Using his uninjured arm, the battered rider rose to his feet and said, ''I hear ya. Maybe you forgot who I work for . . .''

''Nope, and if the Barbed-T wants to make an issue of this, you tell Elam Jordan if he tries to tree South Pass, I'll bring in troops and personally pull the trap door on him.''

The two locked eyes for a long minute, then Bitters turned on his heel and with his back to the marshal, told the third Barbed-T rider, ''Pick up that damn fool kid and bring him along,'' and led the way from the saloon.

Looking up at the shotgunner, Alkire asked, ''Bill, have I got your word this ends here?''

Smaldeen grinned. ''Hell yes. I wasn't gonna cut loose on that gent anyway. I figured if one of those Barbed-T boys tried to come up with a sneak gun or something, I was gonna let daylight through 'em.''

Vent nodded, said, ''Thanks for the kind thoughts,'' and went back to his table and motioning toward an empty chair, waited until the marshal sat down, then reholstered his .44.

A waiter brought a bottle and another glass and left them and Alkire, pouring Vent's glass full and adding a generous shot to his own, lifted it and said, ''To a cold winter, a snug cabin, and a hot-blooded woman,'' and downed it.

Then Vent's food came and he immediately began demolishing it while Alkire watched. Finally, when Vent was wiping up the last of the gravy with a snowflake-light biscuit, he observed, ''Man, you musta been as empty as a swamper's head.''

Catching the waiter's eye, Vent motioned for him to

come over and when he reached the table, told him, "Run that horse around the corral one more time, will ya?"

"How long's it been since you et?" Alkire asked curiously.

Vent grinned. "Not since I left the Platte. Run outa grub and the damned deer and antelope are still down in the low country. Couldn't even spot a mountain goat."

"Hell, no wonder you was so damned touchy about your grub," Alkire said.

Looking around, Vent asked, "How long you been here, Hep?"

"About a year," Alkire replied. "Last marshal wound up on the wrong end of Jess Ewing's gun. He's planted up on the hill."

"Who's here?" Vent asked.

Alkire thought a moment then said, "Isom Dart comes in and out of town and Harvey Logan passed through here with that Parker kid. They was on their way over to Brown's Hole. Masterson rode in and out last year but it's too early for the big money gamblers. Those boys stay in the south until it warms up. . . . You seen Owney Sharp or The Preacher lately?"

Vent moved his used-up dishes to one side as the waiter brought his second helping and then began eating more leisurely as he said, "Owney's down at Crested Butte staying with my sister and her husband. Caught a slug in a fight in Denver."

"I heard about that," Alkire said. "He downed a couple and someone plugged him from behind a door, they say."

Vent grinned. "Yep, and old Owney, he just sorta twisted around and pumped a slug through that door and sent the shooter on his last ride."

"And The Preacher?"

"He's up in Bodie with Arkie Chan. They're partnering in a faro game there," Vent said as he cleaned up the last of his steak.

"You planning on staying around . . . or moving on?" Alkire asked, and Vent knew the marshal didn't want it to sound like he was pushing on Vent to leave town, but he also needed to know what to expect if this man stayed in South Pass City. He was a famed gunman and he had had a run-in with riders from one of the largest ranches on the eastern slope. Either Elam Jordan could elect to forget it, marking it off to Tag Bitters' stupidity, or he could take the tack that nobody manhandles a Barbed-T rider. Whichever way Vent went, Alkire had to know what to expect.

"I'm on my way to Bodie," Vent said and noted the wash of relief move across Alkire's face.

Looking up then, Vent said softly, "No problem, Hep. I stomp my own snakes."

Alkire smiled. "Just wanted to know whether I could expect a long hot summer or not."

"Will the Barbed-T cause you problems over this?" Vent asked.

Alkire shook his head. "Elam knows me and that means he also knows that if he pushes, I'll bring in the Army. He don't want that. He can't win. Elam's a winner."

Finished with his meal, Vent rose and said, "Thanks, Hep, for your help," and walked to the bar and dropped two silver dollars on the plank and left with Alkire trailing him. On the sidewalk the marshal looked at the Appaloosa and said, "I see you've still got the Appy."

Vent nodded. "He's come too far with me now to want anything else."

Upon hearing its master's voice, the horse turned its head and nickered softly. Vent walked to him, pulled up the cinch and stepped into the saddle. Looking down at

Alkire he said, "Watch the alleys, Hep," and rode from South Pass City.

As he put the Appaloosa to the long gentle grade leading westward up and over the Great Divide, he turned in the saddle and looked back at the mean collection of shacks and wondered what possessed folks to settle in such a miserable place. South Pass City had been birthed to the tune of swinging pickaxes and rattling sluice boxes, but now the rich veins of ore were almost played out. Yet men stayed on here, freezing through the bitter winters and half starving in the summers.

Turning back, he looked west and said softly, "Let's get on, horse. It's a long way to Bodie."

Chapter Two

Elam Jordan first appeared on the banks of the Sweetwater River in 1866 when he drove 2,000 head of longhorns over 1,500 miles from south Texas up through the Indian Nations, Kansas, Colorado, and then west to the rich summer ranges of the Great Divide country. He fought Indians, outlaws, herd cutters, and Kansas sodbusters to reach the Sweetwater and, once settled there, carved out a ranch that covered over 100,000 acres of prime grazing land. Where others had lost their herds in the first blizzards and moved on, Elam Jordan stayed. Long before he reached the Sweetwater with his herd, men he had sent on ahead to take and hold the land he prized had cut a huge crop of the wild hay that grew sweet and tall in that country, and had built rough log barns to store it in. When winter tore down from the north to decimate other herds, he had the hay to feed his own and so survived.

At sixty years old, he was still a man from the tip of his bench-made boots to the crown of the black John B. Stetson he sent all the way to Caspar for. There were men who swore they had seen him throw a horse by simply grabbing a handful of mane and the saddle horn and heaving. He was rough, heavy-handed, and illeducated, but considered by those who knew him as a fair man. If he had a fault, it was often misplaced loyalty to his men.

Woe to the man who mistreated a Barbed-T rider. Elam Jordan would not tolerate it and when a man hires and keeps forty hands, he has the guns to make his rules and policies the law in any land. Now he was angry.

Striding up and down the huge front room of the Barbed-T headquarters, his massive head bent forward and his powerful jaw thrust out, he was every inch a man bent on righting what he considered a wrong. Now he whirled and stared at the three punchers sitting in a row on the horse-hide couch and snapped, "There you boys sit; you, Tag, with knots on your head, half your teeth gone, and a busted wing. And you, Kid Calamity," and he paused here and repeated the name and went on, "God knows you're sure as hell named proper, you up and get a toad sticker punched through your paw. Ain't that a hell of a mess? With spring brandin' about to start I got two men laid up because they was damn fools."

"But Mr. Jordan. . . ," Bitters started to speak.

Jordan raised a hand and snarled, "Shut your damn mouth! You, Bobby Bright, you're supposed to be such great shuckins with a handgun; where the hell were you when this ranahan was putting two of my best men out of action?"

Bright, a quiet man with a long face bisected by a brutal nose and a wicked slash of a mouth, said calmly, "Sitting right smack still."

Jordan stared at him. "For God's sake, why?"

"Hell, I ain't ready to croak yet," he replied and began rolling a cigarette.

"I ain't ready to croak yet," Jordan mocked him. "You mean to tell me you were afraid of this feller?"

"You damn betcha, Mr. Jordan. Scared enough to keep my gun in its holster," Bright admitted.

"Who the hell is this gent anyway? Some damn wandering grubliner who's plugged a few swampers and drunks in the back? Hell, them so-called pistol fighters is all alike. They build a big rep on killing helpless folks and a string of their own lies."

"That 'grubliner' you're talking about has killed more than thirty men and nobody ever accused him of putting a drunk in the ground. He's come up against some of the best in the business and they're all wearing a cloud while somebody else forks their saddles."

Jordan stared at him. "What did you say his name was?"

"Vent Torrey, but they call him Leatherhand on account of a leather glove he wears on his right hand," Bright said.

There was one other man in that room and he had remained quietly in a corner while Jordan lambasted his men, but now he spoke up.

"Elam, I know about this feller," Cap Stalls said. Stalls, Jordan's ramrod, was the only man on the ranch who called him by his first name.

Jordan turned and stared at him. "What's so special about him, Cap?" he asked.

Stalls, who was fifty years old and had been up the trail more times than most men could count, said quietly, "Vent Torrey is the last male member of the Torrey family from Missouri. They're feuders. The way the story goes the Torreys and a family named Hawks got into a feud over seventy years ago. Since then they've killed each other on sight. Folks from down in Missouri claim both sides built their own cemetaries. . . ."

Jordan stared at him, then asked curiously, "How many folks got killed off?"

Stalls looked at the three riders sitting on the couch and said quietly, "Over five hundred men have gone down in that feud."

"The hell you say?"

"Yep, and Vent Torrey shot his first Hawks when he was twelve years old. Now the only survivors of both clans is Vent Torrey and Hitch Hawks. Hawks and his sons killed Torrey's paw and two brothers in Kansas and crippled Torrey's gun hand. He left the country and went to Colorado. The Hawks followed him, so the story goes. Out in Colorado, Torrey saved the life of the son of a Ute shaman. The shaman gave Torrey the leather contraption he wears. They say before he had that, he couldn't even use his right hand.

"Anyway, Torrey was barely twenty-one when he tracked down the last of the Hawks and killed them and crippled old Hitch; blew away most of his gun hand, he did . . ."

"He let him go?" Jordan mused.

"He let him go," Stalls said.

Jordan walked to a sideboard and poured himself half a glass of whiskey. He didn't offer any to his men. "Kinda twisty, him nailing the old man in the gun hand after Hawks crippled his gun hand. He more than likely left Hawks alive to see what it was like having a crippled hand. By God, they's a streak of meanness in a man like that. He could have just bumped over old Hawks and ended it."

Stalls nodded agreement. "He could have, but he didn't. Since then he's marshaled around the country, rode shotgun guard and worked undercover for Wells Fargo and the Army . . . and," Stalls stared at the three Barbed-T riders, "he ain't never had the reputation for starting trouble. Just finishing it."

Jordan turned and fastened a pair of winter-cold blue eyes on Bitters and asked softly, "Tag, you certain sure your tripping that waiter was an accident?"

Bitters met the old man's eyes, but it was hard going, and his voice held just the hint of sullenness as he declared, "Yes sir. I didn't set out to do a thing like that."

"Of course not," Jordan remarked. "Hell, you'd never pull a stunt like that 'cause only a damn greenhorn would be so stupid. Besides, if a man deliberately tripped a waiter bringing my dinner, I'd fill the son-of-a-bitch fulla lead and so would most other fellers."

Kid Calamity looked up and said, "Hell, Mr. Jordan, that gent was starting to leave. He was behind us when he just cut loose and wanged Tag in the mouth and pinned my hand to the table with that damned pig sticker. We wasn't doing nothing."

Whether Jordan believed him or not didn't show in his lined face, but then he wouldn't have shown emotion if he were being scalped, and his men knew that.

"You boys say Hep Alkire came in and backed that Torrey gent?"

"Yes sir," Bitters replied. "He just sided right in with him. Looked like he knowed him from somewhere."

Staring at Bitters and The Kid, Jordan said, "You boys get out of here. Stay away from town. I'll have the doc come back out in a week to look you over. You, Bright, hang around," and as the two punchers tramped out, Jordan took a deep pull on his drink and looking at Bright over the rim, asked coldly, "Bobby, what really happened in there?"

Bright hesitated for just a moment, then said positively, "It was like the boys told it, Mr. Jordan."

Turning to Stalls, Jordan said, "Cap, I want you to take Bright here and four more men and bring Mr. Torrey back here. I want his side of this story and if he ain't got one, I'm gonna hang him."

Stalls thought about that for a long minute, then said, "Elam, you ever hear of Owney Sharp or Arkie Chan or Cam Spencer . . . or maybe The Preacher?"

"I've heard of The Preacher, he comes from Texas, and Owney Sharp's been all over hell," Jordan said.

"Well, between Sharp, Arkie Chan, Spencer, The Preacher and Vent Torrey, they've laid down over a hundred men," Stalls told him.

"What's that got to do with this?"

"You hang Leatherhand and you'll have war with the others," Stalls said. "They're all friends and they've all ridden together."

Jordan walked to the window and looked out across the rolling grasslands of the Sweetwater and said, "I've got forty men out there. They all know how to use a gun. I know, 'cause I hired 'em. If the Barbed-T cain't handle a bunch of guntwisters, then it should go under."

Stalls knew discussion was at an end. Rising, he jerked his head at Bright and said, "Let's go, hardcase," and walked to the door where he turned and asked, "How long you want me to keep after this gent?"

" 'Till you find him," Jordan said flatly.

Stalls nodded once and walked out. Bright quietly closed the door behind them.

Vent Torrey rode easy in the saddle as he put the big Appaloosa to the last series of switchbacks in the immigrant trail leading to South Pass, the 7,500-foot cut in the mountains where the Continental Divide lay, an invisible line, athwart the massive string of peaks that divided the

Great Plains from the western territories. Vent had been this way once before and he knew that up there above him somewhere on a wide sweep of top-of-the-world plains was a pile of stones marking the divide. It was here he planned to camp, for those who had gone before had left behind a rock corral, a rough rock lean-to and there was usually a pile of wood for the taking.

As he rounded the last bend, he looked back and far off to the northeast, he could see the glimmer of lights that marked South Pass City and just beyond it, Atlantic City, little more than a store and stage stop. It was Vent's plan to ride over the pass, then drop down and hit Little Sandy Creek, follow it to Green River, and eventually arrive at Rock Springs. From there he would ride south into Colorado and following old Indian trails, work his way south to Crested Butte, to meet up there with Owney Sharp and then ride on to Bodie, California. He was looking forward to visiting the ranch, for he hadn't seen his sister or her husband in well over a year.

Because he was woolgathering, he almost missed seeing the dim glimmer of a campfire up in the pass. When he did spot it, he pulled in his horse and sat looking at the flames for just a minute, then turned off the trail and carefully worked his way around the face of the slope until he reached the top of the pass. Here the ground was flat, stretching away in both directions with nothing to break the monotony except an occasional boulder. From his present position he couldn't see the campfire and guessed it was because the builder had placed it inside the rock shelter and the back wall of the shelter was toward the north, constructed to protect the user from the north winds that often tore across the top of the pass at speeds up to fifty and sixty miles an hour.

Stepping from the saddle, Vent dropped the reins and

walked quietly forward, moving off to the right as he closed the gap between him and the campfire. Then he heard a curse and a grunt. He stopped.

"Old man, you better tell us where you hid that money or I'm gonna cut you sure as I would airy a bull calf," someone said harshly.

"Go to hell," a man answered and the solid crack of a fist on flesh followed.

"Hey, Abe, you take her easy now," another voice warned. "You kill this peckerwood and we'll never find his money."

"Maybe you'd like to try and open his damn mouth," the first man snapped.

"Take it slow, you fellers," a third man spoke. "Hell, he'll tell us. Just give him time," and then Vent was close enough to see what was happening and stopped and watched as the third man drew a huge Bowie knife, leaned over and strapped it on his boot, all the time staring at an older man who lay on the ground tied hand and foot.

Placing all three men, Vent drew his .44 and said quietly, "Howdy, boys. Havin' fun?"

The man with the knife whirled toward Vent as he eared back the hammer of his gun and cursed and then the other two drew and Vent shot them in less than a second, his slugs driving them into the darkness as the third man dropped the Bowie and went for his gun. He made his draw, but died with a slug in his chest long before he could bring the gun into play.

Vent moved ten feet further south and waited. Five minutes crawled by, then he heard someone crawling and heavy breathing and, looking away from the campfire, allowed his eyes to adjust to the darkness and saw the wounded man propped against the side of the lean-to, his gun up and questing for a target.

"Over here," Vent called softly and the man jerked his gun barrel around and fired and the bullet hit a rock and whined viciously away and Vent shot the gunman again, this time putting his bullet half an inch to the right of his left shirt pocket.

The dying man fell sideways with a groan. Vent watched dispassionately as the outlaw raised his legs up against his chest then straightened them out, rolled on his side, and moved no more.

Walking around behind the lean-to, Vent found the third man. He was lying on his back, gun still gripped in his right hand, his eyes wide open and staring unseeingly at the sky.

Knowing he was dead, Vent moved around into the light and, picking up the fallen Bowie knife, leaned over and cut the ropes from the bound man's ankles, then rolled him over and sliced through those holding his wrists.

Stepping back he watched as he sat up and rubbed his right wrist with his left hand, then grinning frostily at Vent, said, "Thanks, friend. They had me going there."

"Glad to help," Vent said and nodding at the coffee, asked, "Mind?"

"Help yourself, you earned it . . ."

Vent squatted and poured coffee into a tin cup he found sitting on a rock, then, looking at the man he had just rescued, said, "I'm Vent Torrey from Missouri."

"Me, I'm Denton Rose. I'm also the damn fool who let those boys sneak up on me and get the drop."

Vent tossed some more wood on the fire then stood up and whistled softly and the Appaloosa came around the shelter, his nostrils flared at the smell of death, and stood looking at his master. Going to the horse, Vent pulled his saddle and bridle and, carrying them to the lean-to, stowed them in a corner and went back to his coffee.

Looking quizzically at the big animal, Rose asked, "Ain't you worried that bugger will run off?"

Vent shook his head. "Nope. The only home he's had for several years has been with me. To him, I'm home. He won't wander off."

As the sticks took flame and the fire grew bigger, Vent had his look at this man he had saved. He saw a man of about fifty-five whose hair had turned white and whose tough, lined face was a road map of years of hard work and no few disappointments. A pair of black, fathomless eyes gave away the fact that somewhere in this man's family tree an ancestor made his home in a squaw's tent, for Indian showed there. His face might have once been handsome but a broken nose poorly healed had taken that away from him, leaving him with a look of tough competence. Vent was surprised such a man could be caught off guard.

When Rose stood up to toss more wood on the fire, Vent saw he was dressed in a worn pair of Levis, a faded gray shirt, and a brown Stetson that had seen more than its share of hard winters. Nearby a pair of batwings lay across a centerfire saddle that had Texas written all over it. The man's gunbelt had been tossed into the back of the lean-to, apparently by his captors, and Vent looked at it and noted the rig was a buscadero belt carrying a Colt .45 Peacemaker in the right hand holster and a .41 Colt Thunderer in the left hand holster. The .41 was holstered so that its butt faced to the front, rather than to the back. A Winchester 44.40 rifle was still in its scabbard on the saddle and Vent wondered why a man would be so careless in this wild place.

"Looks like you weren't expecting trouble," Vent observed.

Rose, who had been watching Vent take his inventory,

said, "Reckon I'm some damn fool. Hell, I know better, too."

"Once in a while a man lets down his guard," Vent said diplomatically.

"And it usually gets him killed," Rose replied, then asked, "You et?"

"Nope," Vent replied, then rose and went to his saddle and dug out bacon and two airtights of peaches. Tossing them to Rose, he said, "You wanta get something going, I'll clear this garbage away from the camp."

While Rose cooked the bacon and made biscuits and gravy, Vent dragged the three corpses off along the slope and left them side by side about fifty yards from the camp. Returning with their gunbelts looped over his shoulders, he tossed them into the lean-to and went to the corral where he found three horses tied. The outlaws hadn't even bothered to loosen the cinches on their saddles. Pulling the rigs from the animals, Vent carried them outside the corral and dropped them on the ground. The old man's horse was staked out near the corral and Vent could hear it tearing up the shallow tufts of bunch grass that grew here so sparsely. The Appaloosa had joined him and the two fed side by side.

Vent came back to camp in time to start on the first batch of biscuits and gravy and while he ate, Rose cooked. When Vent finished, Rose ate and Vent cooked the seconds. The rough meal completed, Vent used his knife to open the airtights and handing one to Rose, said, "I been thinking about these for a month. I bought them just before I rode out of South Pass City."

Eating the peaches and relishing every bite, Vent nodded toward the outlaws' horses and observed, "Reckon if a man turned them old ponies loose, they'd head right back for home. I figure them pistoleros up and borrowed them somewhere."

"Well, I reckon we can turn 'em loose in the morning," Rose suggested.

Vent, dog-tired, agreed then digging out a silver dollar, said, "Match you for first guard duty," and flipped the coin and lost.

At midnight Vent shook Rose awake and watched as the older man got up and painfully hobbled around strapping on his gunbelt and pulling his rifle from its scabbard. Noticing Vent watching him, he grinned sourly. "Feller gets my age, he begins to feel every broken bone or hurt he ever had."

"Age ain't got nothing to do with it, Mr. Rose," Vent said and rolled up in his blanket and was almost immediately asleep. He awoke instantly to Rose's touch and took the two to four guard mount, then watched Rose walk out into the night and take up his station behind a large boulder.

Vent awoke with the sun in his face and knew instantly he was not alone and that it wasn't Rose who watched him. Opening his eyes just a slit, he saw half a dozen horsemen sitting their mounts thirty feet away and wondered why Rose hadn't warned him.

One of them rode forward and said casually, "Just as well open your eyes, mister. Playing possum ain't gonna keep the rope from around your neck."

Vent rolled over then and lifted the .44 and centered it on the man's chest, saw the badge there and kept the gun rock steady.

"Hell, mister, you can't take us all," the lawman said reasonably.

Rising slowly, Vent leaned against the rocky shelter wall and had his look at the mounted men and saw they all wore badges and thought, Jordan's sent a posse after me, and still holding the gun centered on the sheriff's chest, asked, "You mentioned hanging. You figure on making me the guest of honor?"

"What else would a feller do with a horse thief?" the sheriff asked reasonably.

Vent grinned. "Why you'd up and hang him, of course."

"Glad you agree. Me, I'm Sheriff Bade Williams, I'm kinda what passes for law around here," the lawman said.

One of the deputies dropped a hand casually onto his thigh inches away from his gunbutt and Vent, watching the movement from the corner of his eye, asked the sheriff, "What's that boy's name wearing the yeller scarf?"

"What? Oh, that's Cal Turner, my deputy. Why?"

"Just like to know who I bump off and he's next on the list if he don't take his hand away from that gun," Vent explained quietly.

"What's your name?" Williams asked.

"Name's Vent Torrey from Missouri," Vent said and watched the deputy jerk his hand away from his gun, a movement the sheriff didn't miss.

Glancing around at Turner, Williams asked, "You know this here grubliner?"

"He ain't no grubliner, Bade. That's Leatherhand we got there," Turner said.

Looking at the rock-steady .44 in Vent's hand, Williams said ruefully, "I reckon they just might be some question as to who has who."

"I don't think they's any question about it," Denton Rose said, and the cocking of the rifle he leveled across the rock where he had been hiding was loud on the clear mountain air.

"Whipsawed," the sheriff said bitterly.

"Pretty sloppy law work, Mr. Williams," Vent observed.

Placing both hands on the saddle horn, the sheriff lowered his chin on his chest and remained motionless for a long moment then looked up at Vent and said, "I suppose you got some explanation for those horses you got penned up over there?"

Vent nodded. "Yep, sure do. In the first place, I didn't pen them up. Neither did Mr. Rose; that's the feller over there with the rifle, but if one of your boys will ride out behind the lean-to here, he'll find three men who did leave them there."

Nodding at one of the deputies, Williams said, "Go check," and waited until the man rode over, had his look at the bodies, and rode back.

Looking at him, Williams asked, "Well?"

"Spud Hanley, Bart Talbert, and Indian Billy are laying over there all shot to hell," the deputy said.

"You did for them?" Williams asked.

"I did," Vent admitted. "Rode in here last night and they had Mr. Rose tied hand and foot and were fixing to peel off his hide with a Bowie. Figured he had money hid somewhere around here. I sorta took a hand and they went to the gun. I killed them."

"Heard you was kinda sudden," Williams said.

"What was you planning on doing with them horses?" one of the deputies inquired.

"Turn them loose. Figured they'd go home . . ."

"Well, seeing as they're all stolen from ranches around here, I reckon they would have . . . Mr. Torrey, I've heard you're a fair and honest man; heard you done some lawing your ownself; also heard you don't hire your gun. I'm inclined to believe that, seeing as how it was told me by Hep Alkire. I always respected Mr. Alkire . . ."

Vent nodded and holstered his gun. Looking at Williams he asked, "You boys join us for breakfast?"

Williams looked around at his posse and grinned. "We'll join you, but I reckon we better furnish our own chuck or you fellers are gonna have to live on mighty slim rations until you hit the next supply stop. These old boys know how to eat,'' and he stepped off his horse and came over and extended his hand.

Vent shook it and then Rose came in, carrying his rifle under his arm, nodded to the posse and, leaning the rifle against the rock wall, began bustling around the fire as Vent said, ''Mr. Denton Rose here, he's the best damn camp cook I ever met.''

''Reckon we'll test his wind,'' Williams said as his men began digging food from their saddlebags.

After the posse had eaten, they saddled the three stolen horses, draped the rapidly stiffening bodies over them and lashed them in place. Staring at them Williams observed, ''Those old boys weren't very damn pretty when they were alive and catching a bad case of death sure as hell didn't improve their looks.''

''They wanted for anything?'' Rose asked.

''Oh, I reckon I can find half a dozen dodgers on these boys if I go digging through my desk,'' Williams said, then mounting his horse, nodded at Vent and Rose and said quietly, ''Mr. Torrey, I heard me a little rumor back in South Pass City. Seems as how Elam Jordan has tolled off five of his men and put Cap Stalls, his segundo, in charge. They got orders to bring you back for a hanging.''

Shaking his head, Vent observed, ''Folks around here sure as hell seem to have a close working relationship with hemp rope.''

''Hell, we ain't got much choice,'' Williams said. ''That jail in South Pass City wouldn't hold a drunk Paiute. Seems as how if they's any justice to be had, it's at the end of a rope.''

Rose smiled frostily, observing, ''One thing about

hanging; it sure as hell chokes off any objections a feller might have.''

Chuckling, Williams turned his horse and led his men down the mountain.

He did not look back.

Cap Stalls had worked for Elam Jordan for fifteen years. He respected and was loyal to the old man, even when he disagreed with him, for he did not believe in taking a man's money and then standing against him. If ever the day came when he could no longer ride the same trail Jordan chose, then Stalls knew he would ride out.

He wasn't a man that folks noticed straight off, unless it was to take in the fact that Stalls only stood five foot six in his high-heeled boots and weighed less than 150 pounds. He was possessed of one of those young-old faces that made it difficult to guess his age and Stalls had never told anyone, including Elam Jordan, how old he was. He considered that information his own.

Women looked past him the first time around, but then after taking a second look, they usually discovered something in Stalls that attracted them, even though they could not say what it was. His face was cherubic and men who didn't like the Barbed-T ramrod had been heard to remark that he should have been a church usher rather than the riding boss of a 100,000-acre ranch boasting a forty-man crew.

However, there were other men around the eastern slope country that could attest to the fact that a light-complected face and mild blue eyes didn't necessarily mean the owner of same was a gent just any man could walk over. Neither did prematurely white hair.

Stalls could literally whip his weight in wildcats and he was far better with the short-barreled sheriff's model .45

Colt he wore than the average puncher. If he had been a man to carve notches, he could have cut six in the butt plates of his pistol.

Those who knew him left him alone.

Now he sat his horse on a high bank above a small pond and watched three of his riders push a handful of cattle away from a quicksand bog on the south side of the lake and chase them up and out of the hollow. One of the riders, a tall, easy-riding man wearing batwings, a heavy cowhide jacket lined with wool, and a battered Texas hat, its wide brim slanted over his eyes, looked up and seeing Stalls, came along the bank, his legs thrust into sheepskin-lined taperderos that almost dragged the ground. The big double-rigged saddle he rode made the tough little buckskin it sat on look even smaller than it was.

Pulling up, the tall man grinned around a neatly clipped mustache and, hooking a leg over the horn, began rolling a cigarette.

"Roy, you come along with me," Stalls directed. "Got a special job the old man wants done," and without further explanation turned his grulla and rode north.

A two-hour ride put them on the edge of a meadow where a small corral sitting next to a rough log-line shack held four horses. As they rode in and dismounted, a dark-complected man showing enough Indian blood to make it easy to recognize him as a halfbreed, stepped from the cabin and, leaning against a porch support, said with a grin, "Damn, caught me in the act. Here I just got done cooking up some Barbed-T beef and along comes the ramrod."

Stalls looked at him and then glancing at his companion, said, "Roy, ain't that just like a damned breed to up and admit he's a cow thief?"

Roy Powers, looking solemn, suggested, "Maybe we

best go in and check this beef out just to make certain it's Barbed-T beef. Hell, as slick as this here gent is, he could easily have downed one of the Rocking A outfit's cows.''

''Good idea,'' Stalls agreed and loosening the cinch, he ground tied his horse and followed Powers inside where they found a large plate of steaks sitting on the warming tray of the stove.

''Got any biscuits, mister rustler?'' Powers asked.

''Yep,'' the halfbreed said laconically and opening the oven, pulled forth a pan full of them and, using a spatula, ladeled them onto a dish, set out the steaks and, distributing dishes around the table, stood back and waited.

Looking the table over, Stalls shook his head. ''You know, Mr. Powers, I was inclined to go easy on this here rustler until I seen they ain't no gravy . . .''

Wordlessly, the halfbreed went to the stove and brought a frying pan to the table and sat it down on a piece of board. It was full to the rim with meat gravy.

''He's out of the woods,'' Stalls said and without another word the three men fell to.

Hance Hall's mother was a full-blooded Comanche and his father a black Irishman with a vicious temper when drunk, a line of blarney when sober, and a pair of fists that had leveled half the male population of Guthrie, Oklahoma before a wet-eared gunsel emptied a shotgun into his chest one night over a dancehall girl and wound up the honored guest at a necktie party.

Hance had been eighteen years old when Kevin Hall was buried in the Guthrie boothill. His mother returned to the Comanche tribe and Hance saddled a broken-down plow horse and rode west. Two days out of Guthrie, he trapped a speckle-butted stud in a blind canyon, roped it, and rode it into the ground. When all the buck was out of it, he turned its head west and leaving the plowhorse to fatten on the buffalo grass, rode away.

Hall at eighteen was a lean whiplash of a man with startling gray eyes in a dark face, crowned by an unruly mop of black hair. Like most men of his day, he wore a gun, but preferred a knife. The cold feel of the steel gave him a surge of almost perfect euphoria and the two men who had decided to test his ability with it had died as quickly as if they had been shot. In both instances the tribal police in the Indian Nations ruled self-defense and marked young Hall as a man to watch.

He rode for half a dozen outfits until Elam Jordan hired him to twist broncs. That had been three years ago and Hall was still doing it. The four horses out in the corral were in various stages of being broken, as he used them riding line.

The men liked him and so did Jordan. Hall didn't think he would ever leave the Barbed-T, although he had never said so in that many words. Now he pushed his plate back and, pouring his cup full of coffee from the blackened pot, rolled a cigarette and said, "Now that you boys have et up my month's ration of grub, maybe you'll tell me what brings you out this way."

Cap Stalls, rolling his own smoke, looked at Hall and said, "The old man's got a little chore for us. Want you to bring your ponies into the home ranch and turn them over to Rafferty and be ready to ride out in the morning. Get your gear in shape and draw some extra rifle and handgun shells from Cookie."

Hall lit his cigarette and gazed at Stalls, then asked quietly, "We going to war?"

"I'll fill you in just before we leave," Stalls promised. "They'll be you, me, and four other Barbed-T riders," and he rose and went out and cinched up his horse and he and

Powers mounted. Sitting deep in the saddle, Stalls looked down at Hall and observed, "That beef, it sure as hell wasn't Barbed-T. Not tasty enough," and he wheeled his horse and led Powers away from the line shack at a run.

Stalls' next stop was on the northwest range, where he found five men sitting around a chuck wagon eating. Nearby three more rode circle on two hundred longhorns, each with a calf or calves at its side. This was a spring branding crew and when Stalls and Powers rode in, the foreman stood up and waited for Stalls to dismount, then pointed to the coffee pot and said, "She's good and hot, Cap."

Cap Stalls liked Elm Landers. He was a top-notch cowman and had a knack for handling men. Now he walked over and poured coffee into a tin cup the cook handed him and, looking into the foreman's eyes, said, "Elm, the old man's sending me and some of the boys west on a special deal. While I'm gone you'll act as ramrod. Check with Elam as soon as this gather is branded."

Looking puzzled, Landers asked, "Mind telling a feller what's going on?"

"Elam'll do that," Stalls promised, then glancing around, asked, "Where's Jeff Kidder?"

"Out with the herd," Landers said. "You want him?"

Turning to Powers, Stalls nodded toward the herd and ordered, "Go fetch Kidder, will you, Roy?"

Powers turned his horse and rode into the darkness, returning in a few minutes followed by a neatly dressed youth whose short hair and clean-shaven face contrasted sharply with the rest of the crew's appearance.

A former scout for the Seventh Cavalry, Kidder had fought in half a dozen skirmishes with the plains tribes and all before he was twenty. Just twenty-two now, he nonetheless had the respect of every man on the Barbed-T. There

was little to mark him different. He wore Levis, chaps, a
fleece-lined jacket, half-boots adorned with long-shanked
spurs and a flat-crowned gambler's hat. At his hip a single
shell belt held two seven-and-one-half-inch barrel .45 Colt
Army issue single actions, butt forward.

Now he dropped from his horse and, grinning at Stalls,
asked, "You gonna give me notice or just tie the can on
me?"

"You do something you figure you deserve to be fired
for?" Stalls asked.

"Hell yes, but now I'm wondering which deal it was
you found out about," Kidder responded.

"You gonna fess up?" Stalls asked, looking at Kidder
narrowly.

"Not on your tintytype, I ain't. Mrs. Kidder didn't fetch
up no idiots, nor damn fools, for that matter."

Stalls refilled his coffee cup and observed, "Well, in
that case, I guess we'll just forget the whole thing and
instead, you're elected to come along with me and Powers
and a couple of the other boys on a special job the old man
wants done."

Elm Landers came over and smiling, said, "Don't worry
none about that schoolmarm you been sparkin' over to
Green River, old son. Me, I'll be more than happy to go
on over there and cut her kindling for her."

"More like go over and get his saddle horn polished,"
Powers observed.

Kidder shook his head. Looking at Stalls, he asked,
"Can you tally that? This old boy actually thinkin' he
could just waltz over there and beat my time? I ain't
worried."

"In that case, cut a fresh horse and let's ride," Stalls
ordered.

When Stalls led Powers and Kidder into the home ranch,

he found Elam Jordan sitting in an old rocker on the front veranda, his scarred boots up on the rail, a drink in his hand and a good cigar clamped between his teeth. He was bareheaded, but wore a gun. Sitting beside him was a tall, clean-shaven man wearing black from the crown of his John B. to the tip of the bench made boots he wore. A mass of almost white hair that hung to his shoulders and a pair of cold green eyes clashed almost violently with his outfit.

Dismounting, Stalls handed the reins to Powers and, without looking around, ordered, "Put these horses in the barn and then I want you two, and Hance and Bobby, to come up here to the house."

Stalls climbed the four steps to the veranda, and leaning against a rail, looked at the black-clad man and said, "Howdy, Whitey. How you?"

"As well as any man could expect, given the circumstances," Whitey Beard answered.

Stalls did not like Beard. There was something about the easterner that rubbed him wrong. Maybe it was the assurance; Beard always seemed to be in total control. Stalls had never seen him rattled. And, he could use the twin .44s he carried in a single belt worn high around his waist. Stalls rated Beard as the best man with a handgun he had on the Barbed-T and he knew he was perfect for this job, but that didn't mean he had to like the man.

Elam Jordan pushed a chair around with his boot toe and said, "Sit, you look tuckered," and when Stalls sat down, the old man looked at him keenly and observed, "Bright, Powers, Hall, Kidder, and Mr. Beard, here. The best men I've got on the spread. I just hope to hell we don't get hit by Injuns or rustlers while you're gone."

"We'll need the best," was all Stalls said, then his picked crew came straggling up from the bunkhouse and

Stalls looked at Jordan and asked, "You gonna tell 'em or you want me to?"

Jordan stood up. "I'll tell them," he said and when the men stopped in the yard and waited, watching the old man, he took his time looking them over and decided if they couldn't get the job done, nobody could.

"Boys, couple days ago Bitters, Bobby Bright and Kid Calamity went into South Pass City for a drink or two," and he looked out over their heads and inserted, "More like a dozen or so," and chuckles answered this sally as he continued, "Anyway, they was a gent in the Silver Dollar, a drifter passing through, and he ordered a meal. When the waiter brought it he fell . . . fell over Bitters' foot . . ."

The men looked at each other, but nobody smiled.

Jordan gave them time to comment and when they didn't, went on, "This feller didn't like his dinner tossed on the floor, so he ups and pulls a hogleg and busts out a few of Bitters' teeth and when The Kid tries to buy in, pins his hand to the table with a toad sticker . . ."

Now he had their attention.

"Hep Alkire waltzed in about that time and he sided with the stranger," Jordan said. There was no bitterness in his voice. "Hep's a damn good lawman and belongs to no man. That's why I brought him in. He was doing what he thought best. . . .

"Now, this gent rode west. I've only heard our side. I want to hear his . . ."

"Who is this feller?" Kidder asked quietly.

"He's a man they call Leatherhand, but his name's Vent Torrey," Jordan said and watched his men's faces.

There was a sound of movement behind him and Jordan turned and found Beard staring at him. "Something wrong, Whitey?" Jordan asked.

"Oh nothin'," Beard said, adding, "Leatherhand's just about the fastest man with a gun alive today."

Still staring at the easterner, Jordan asked quietly, "You're saying you couldn't beat him in a standup fight?"

Beard smiled. "That remains to be seen, but from what I've heard about Leatherhand, you'd best send a lot more men than this. Hell, he'll eat these boys for breakfast . . ."

Looking at the men Jordan asked, "Anybody else here know anything about this gun whiz?"

Jeff Kidder looked up from the ground and said quietly, "I know him. He's always been a squareshooter, but he's chain lightning when he's crowded into a fight. Whitey's right. He's damn fast . . ."

Staring at them, Jordan said, "You're the best I've got. I'm not sending you out to get yourselves killed. I want this Leatherhand back here alive."

"What if he don't want to come back?" Bright asked.

Jordan looked at the man for a long moment, then said quietly, "It'll be you boys' job to see that he does . . . and Bobby, if he agrees to come back and you've lied to me, you best keep on riding . . ."

Bright looked away.

Jordan nodded at Stalls and turned and went into the house. Stalls, hands on hips, looked down at the men then said, "Pick out the best trail horses in the string and two packers. Hance, go over to the kitchen and have Cookie give you grub for two weeks, then you boys get your gear together and get it on the packers . . . and plan for a long ride. We may be gone all summer," and he followed Jordan inside.

The old man was sitting in a chair before the fireplace staring into the flames when Stalls came and sat down on the hearth. "We'll need money," he said.

"In the office. Get whatever you figure you'll need," Jordan told him.

Stalls went to the office and returned with a handful of bills and said, "I've drawn a thousand. Figure I may have to buy some information along the way," then he looked at Jordan sharply and observed, "You ain't too certain sure of this thing, are you?"

"Hell, I figure all three of those boys are lying, but they's only one way to prove it; ask Leatherhand."

"You could get some of us killed," Stalls pointed out.

Jordan grinned wickedly then, and replied, "Make sure it's Bright, will you?"

Chapter Three

Vent and Rose made good time on the western slope of the Rockies. They dropped down a winding trail marked by the heavy wheels of hundreds of immigrant wagons and on some of the rougher stretches saw evidence that more than one of those wagons hadn't made it. They lay beside the road, canted at awkward angles, the canvas long since rotted away. Here the trail dropped west by easy stages and, once when they rode out along a stringer ridge, they saw half a dozen Indians disappear down a draw a mile north of them and pulled up and waited to see if they would turn back. Half an hour later, the same band appeared briefly riding along a rocky ridge and then disappeared again around a point of rock. They did not reappear.

Far to the west Vent could just make out the Eden Valley and to the north the ragged wasteland that was the Wind River Range thrusting its peaks to the sky. It was along their tops the Continental Divide showed on maps, but Vent had heard the line hadn't as yet been surveyed and wondered how anyone could positively say it was actually the absolute top of the world.

Looking north, Vent was awed by the majestic splendor of mighty Gannett Peak, thrusting over 13,000 feet into the clouds and considered the highest point in Wyoming Territory.

Pointing to it, Vent asked Rose, "How'd you like to be on top of that bugger in nothin' but your longjohns?"

Rose grinned. "Mr. Torrey, you sure as hell can come up with some humdingers."

They were riding along a gentle slope where the wild hay reached to their stirrups and deer grazed within easy rifle shot of them, only occasionally looking up, then going back to their feeding. Once they watched a herd of elk feeding in a mountain pond where beaver had dammed a small stream. High in the rocks, mountain goats and sheep ran along ledges and leaped escarpments that made Vent dizzy just to look at.

"Hell of a country," he observed.

Rose nodded. "One of the best spring ranges in the west, but the winters can sure as hell get rough here, so I've been told."

"Mr. Rose, it ain't polite to ask a man where he's headed, but I figure maybe you might let me know how much longer I can expect to enjoy your company if it don't fuss you none," Vent invited suddenly.

Rose smiled and looking around at Vent, said, "I got me a son. He worked a ranch with me back in Texas . . . east Texas. We got into an argument and Carroll, he just rode out. Broke his maw's heart, he did. She up and died last winter and I didn't have the spunk to keep on running the old place so I sold it."

Vent nodded. It was a story that had been told a hundred times around chuck wagon fires. A man loses his son one way or another and sells his ranch and starts drifting. Works where he can find it. Always a good hand, he fits on any ranch, but his heart has left him and he don't give a damn. Vent had met his share of such men.

"Well, I drifted around some, then I begun hearing these stories; how a young feller named Carroll Rose was building a big rep with a gun. I started lookin' for him. I been down into New Mexico and Nevada and all over Colorado and Kansas."

"No word on him, huh?" Vent asked.

"Plenty of word," Rose said bitterly. "I been following that boy by the dead men he's left behind. So far he's put seven men under ground."

"Hired gun?" Vent inquired, his voice neutral.

Rose shook his head. "That, I could understand. Nope, he just bumps 'em off for fun, so they say. Gambles for a living and cheats and when someone has the guts to call him, why, wang! He ups and plugs the poor feller."

"Hell of a note," Vent observed.

Rose pulled in his horse and looked at Vent for a long time, then said quietly, "Vent, I know you never hire your gun, but I'd like to hire it."

Vent looked away then back at Rose and asked, "What for?"

"I want you to cripple my son," Rose said flatly.

"The hell you say?"

Rose looked into Vent's eyes and said coldly, "I didn't raise my boy to kill innocent folks. He was raised a Christian, just like his maw and me. Hell, I ain't perfect and I don't always do unto others as I'd have them do unto me, but I don't shoot folks for fun neither."

Hooking his knee around the saddle horn, Vent dug out tobacco, rolled a cigarette, and handed the sack to Rose. Lighting up, he watched the old man put his own smoke together and noticed he was having a hard time manipulating his hands and asked, "You got the rumatiz?"

Rose nodded disgustedly. "Kinda slows me up sometimes. You see, it was me who taught Carroll how to use a gun."

"You want me to cripple his gun arm? Is that it?"

Rose looked at him then down at Vent's leather covered right hand and said, "Maybe you're the wrong man to ask that of. Hell, a feller who's had his wing cropped sure knows what it's all about."

Vent thought about the months of agony he had suffered as a result of the Hawks bullet he had taken through his hand and said quietly, "You realize that if I put your boy out of action, every flash gunman around will be out to carve his notch?"

"I've got me a bit of money," Rose said. "Those boys back there at the pass musta found out some way that I sold my ranch. I usually hide the money when I make camp at night. It was hid last night, but they's enough left to start another spread. I figure if Carroll can't use that gun anymore, he'll come home. . . ."

Vent thought he no longer had the ability to feel compassion for any man, but suddenly he hurt for this man who only wanted a son back and was so desperate to force his return he would even pay to have him crippled.

Taking a deep breath and dropping his foot into the stirrup, he said, "Mr. Rose, I admire what you're trying to do. It won't work. A man has to want to come home and even a bullet can't force him."

Rose looked toward the towering monstrosity of Gannett Peak and asked quietly, "What the hell am I going to do?"

"I'll help you find the boy," Vent promised. "Then we see. Just maybe he'll come back with you anyway. Things have a way of working themselves out."

They left it there and rode on and that night they camped

on the banks of the Big Sandy and the next day made Eden, north of Rock Springs, at noon. Leaving the horses at the livery to be grained and rubbed down, they hunted up a restaurant and ordered steak, eggs, and potatoes, and a big pot of coffee.

Eden resembled a thousand such overnight mining camps that had sprung up in the wake of gold or silver discoveries, then, when the veins started playing out, were left near-ghost towns as the fortune seekers went on to the next strike.

Vent looked around as they walked out on the rough wooden sidewalk then turned and nodding at a saloon, asked Rose, "A drink?"

The ex-rancher said, "The seat of all knowledge," and followed Vent into a place called Eden's Retreat.

Sitting at a table against the wall, Vent inventoried the place, noting the elderly swamper washing down spittoons in the back of the room, the thin bartender wearing the bowler hat, and the usual polyglot of customers ranking from a gambler holding sway at a faro layout to a couple of hard-bitten punchers drinking beer at the bar.

The bartender held up a whiskey bottle and Vent nodded and he came around the plank and set two glasses on their table, poured them full and said boredly, "Fifty cents," and Vent paid and said, "Leave the bottle," and the apron hesitated, then looked into the tall young man's eyes and set the jug down and went away.

They had their drink and a refill and Vent returned the bottle, paid another fifty cents and leaning on the bar, asked the bartender, "Looking for a young feller. Name's Carroll Rose. Does a little gambling."

The bartender froze, then in a quick shifty move of his eyes, looked past Vent at the card table and back again and said, "He was here. Left a dead man to mark his passing."

Vent had been watching the faro layout and now he turned as the dealer rose and came to stand in front of Vent. "You looking for Carroll Rose?"

"That's right," Vent said, noting the man had his hand hooked in his belt, but didn't appear to be wearing a gun. Shoulder holster, he thought.

"Why?"

Vent smiled. "None of your damn business," and he looked the gambler in the eyes and waited, his hands crossed over his chest.

"You're kinda unfriendly, ain't ya?" the gambler asked.

"I'm gonna get a damn sight more unfriendly if you try for the shoulder rig you're wearing," Vent warned.

The gambler frowned, then said quietly, "Mister, I can spot you and your friend there a good two seconds and kill you both."

Rose started grinning, then suddenly began to laugh and turning, he pounded his fist on the bar and roared with laughter as the saloon crowd stared in open-mouthed amazement.

"What's so damned funny?" the gambler asked, his face turning red.

Rose turned around then and managed to stop laughing as he said, "You, mister, you're funny."

"Well, old man, laugh this off," the gambler snarled and went for his gun.

Vent's hand snapped down and came up filled with .44 while the gambler's hand was still inside his coat. He froze as Vent set the barrel beneath his chin and said softly, "If I was you, I'd haul that hand out of there empty."

Suddenly the bartender said, "Ramp, do what he says. That's Leatherhand."

Looking along the gun barrel at Vent's leather covered hand, the gambler's face slowly turned white and he swallowed and said distinctly, "I don't suppose an apology would help?"

"An explanation would go further," Vent said as the man brought his empty hand from beneath his coat and held both arms wide of his body.

"I . . ." the gambler started to explain when the door opened and a man wearing a marshal's badge strode in, stopped and looked at Vent and said, "Here now, cowboy, you take that there pistolo outa old Ramp's guzzle and come along to jail with me."

Rose stared at him, then drew swiftly, aligned his gun barrel on the marshal's chest and said, "This damn town's full of comedians."

Staring at Rose the marshal said belligerently, "Hey now, mister, you can go to jail with your friend, you know?"

Without looking at the marshal, Vent said, "Denton, if that mouth says another word, close it permanently," and with his gun barrel still under the gambler's chin, ordered, "Let's hear it."

Taking a deep breath, which only served to make him feel the gun barrel more, he said, "This kid Carroll Rose came to town and got into a poker game here. My brother was in that game. Bill caught Rose cheating and called him. Rose shot and killed Bill. I wasn't here, but they say he's a gunfighter . . . just like you, Mr. Leatherhand."

Nodding at Ramp's coat, Vent observed, "Seems to me you kinda fancy yourself one, too."

"I'm good, but I ain't in your class," he answered.

Vent dropped his gun in his holster and, walking over to the marshal, said, "Marshal, my name's Vent Torrey from Missouri. The gentleman holding on you is Denton Rose.

He's looking for his son. The boy apparently got himself into a shooting here. I don't know the why of it or who was in the wrong or right. None of my put in. Ramp there, he lost a brother. Reckon he figured if we was young Rose's friends, we was fair game. Had to get that notion outa his head. Reckon he sees the light now.''

Glancing nervously at Rose the marshal said, ''In that case I see no reason to bother you fellers. How about you tell that gent to point that cannon some other direction?''

Rose looked at Vent and when Vent nodded, reholstered his gun and turning to the bartender, said, ''Set the house up and give us one for the road . . . and oh yes, mister gambler, what direction did you say Carroll Rose rode in?''

The gambler cleared his throat and it was obvious he didn't like it, but he finally said, ''I heard he headed for Rock Springs.''

Vent and Rose had their drink and quietly left the saloon, walking past the marshal, who still stood in the middle of the bar room digesting the fact that he had just ordered the fastest gunfighter in the western states to put away his pistol and come to jail.

In the next three weeks, Vent and Rose visited four towns and in each town were told that young Rose had passed through, stopping briefly to make his mark at the poker table. He always won.

Then a liveryman at Bonanza, Utah told Vent that Carroll Rose had been in that town for two days, had played poker, and sparked a local girl. When one of her four brothers objected, young Rose smiled at him and killed him on the main street while half the town and the girl looked on, then mounted the big gray stud he rode and left town at a leisurely gallop.

''Any idea where he was heading?'' Vent had asked.

"Told me he left some unfinished business in Rock Springs," the man had said, so now Vent and Rose were riding back into Wyoming.

They hit town late that evening and stabled their horses and went to the nearest eating place, ate a late supper, then drifted along the main drag. Located in the high country near the upper end of Flaming Gorge, Rock Springs had seen its share of the wild ones.

It was a coal mining town with a mixed population, starting life as a stage stop on the Overland Trail and had taken its name from a spring in the area. As the two men rode into town, a sign informed them the place had been incorporated in 1868 and Vent, looking at it, said, "I hear the Union Pacific owns just about the whole town."

"It ain't much of a town," Rose observed, nodding at another sign that informed visitors the present population stood at 770 people.

Vent noted the railroad ran through the center of the place with a street paralleling it on each side of the right-of-way. Houses were scattered around in a random fashion, many of them crude shacks built from old tin, mining timbers, boards salvaged God only knew where, and sheets of canvas.

Riding down the main street, Vent noticed a creek running through town. It was still up due to winter melt off in the hills, but the extra water couldn't hide the fact Rock Springs' citizens were using it as a convenient sewer.

Glancing toward the creek, Rose said disgustedly, "That's what I always liked about towns; they smell so clean."

The country surrounding Rock Springs was about as unprepossessing as the town itself, with the exception of the oddly shaped rock formations that occasionally cropped up. Their pinnacles thrust thirty and forty feet into the sky and the few trails and roads in the area wound their way through them like snake tracks. Although the elevation was over six thousand feet, the country was flat for the most part and the only vegetation worth noting was sagebrush, which grew in profusion.

Looking around him at the town and the barren country stretching away east, Vent shook his head and observed, "Why a man would come all the way from the east to waller around in a black pit for coal in a place like this beats hell outa me."

They found a livery and stabled their horses and went in search of a meal. Sitting in a small cafe and being served by a Swedish girl who spoke only broken English and, listening to the cook, who was German, giving her orders, made the two men wonder where the hell they were.

"This here place sure does have a bunch of foreigners in it, don't it?" Rose noted.

"I heard once they was fifty-six different nationalities here," Vent remarked, then something a miner at the next table said to his eating companion caught Vent's attention. The man had spoken just loudly enough for Vent to over-hear him. "They say them fellers come from east of the divide. They're on a manhunt. Trying to come up on a gent named Torrey. Big rancher over there wants him . . ."

The other miner, his mouth full of food, asked, "Where they staying?"

"At the Green River House," the first miner answered and stuffed steak into his mouth.

Rose had also been listening and now he glanced at Vent and raised a quizzical eyebrow, but said nothing. They finished the meal and walked out onto the sidewalk, where Vent paused and had his look along the street. Glancing at Rose, he said, "Denton, if you wanta ride out now, I'll not take offense. This here's my fight."

"Now that's a hell of a thing to say to me," Rose

complained. "Here you was riding along with me helping to find my boy and you sure as hell didn't have to buy that kinda trouble, but you did."

"Then I reckon I owe you an explanation," Vent said. Leading the way down street, they turned along the first alley they came to and walked to the banks of the Green River where Vent sat down and leaned against the butt of a tree. Rose sat on a stump and rolled a cigarette, offered his tobacco to Vent and, when the Missourian shook his head, pocketed it.

"I stopped in South Pass City for a meal and tangled with some fellers who work for the Barbed-T. Had to pistol-whip one gent and then some damn kid tried to throw down on me and I sorta pinned his hand to the table with my sticker. Reckon it made the owner of the Barbed-T mad as hell . . ."

Rose grinned. "I can see how he wouldn't cotton to having two of his men put outa action just at the beginning of spring gather. I know old Elam Jordan. He's a damn tough man, but he's also a fair one."

"Well, according to Williams, he's sent six men after me," Vent said. "The sheriff claimed Jordan wants me back there as the honored guest at a hanging."

"How come you to tangle with them in the first place?"

"One of them, an ugly jasper with mean written all over him—they called him Bitters—tripped a waiter who was bringing my supper. Feller dumped the whole damn thing in the sawdust. Me, I hadn't eaten for two days and it sorta galled me . . ."

Rose laughed. "I'd see how it would. That feller Bitters, he do the trippin' on purpose?"

"Yep, even laughed about it and turned around and gave me the eye with fight written all over him. Reckon he was just feelin' mean or the likker was doing his thinking."

"More than one man went down because of that master," Rose observed.

"That's a true story," Vent agreed.

Mashing his cigarette out in the dirt, Rose inquired, "Now what?"

"We find your boy first, then I figure to pay a call on Elam Jordan, only it won't be in front of any man's gun," Vent said coldly.

The big, slovenly miner stared across the felt-covered table at the slim, smiling boy in the fancy duds and took an instant dislike to him. He had just sat down and the miner, looking him over, figured he was a dead beat on the fly and vowed that the first bad move the angel-faced kid with the gold curls hanging down to his shoulders made, he, Big Al Kalmikov, would stick his knife right smack dab in the peckerwood's guzzle.

"Cards, gentlemen," the dealer intoned and the kid, under the gun, asked for two. The man next to him wanted three and the next man, a coal-dobbed tunnel rat, asked for one. Kalmikov took two. He held three kings.

The tunnel rat bet five dollars and Kalmikov, deciding to test the fancy kid's wind, upped it fifty dollars and grinned in the boy's face. Smiling serenely, the kid saw the fifty and raised it a hundred. The man behind him tossed in his cards with a disgusted grunt and Kalmikov, looking at his hand again and smiling inwardly at the four big kings lying there in a row, grunted, "The price of poker has just gone up," and bet two hundred after meeting the kid's bet.

The tunnel rat looked at his cards again and said disgustedly, "Now what the hell am I doing in here?" and tossed in.

The kid, still smiling, called Kalmikov's bet and upped him another two hundred. Staring across the table the big miner wondered what the hell the boy had caught, then decided he was bluffing and called him.

"Read 'em and weep," the kid said and fanned four aces flat on the felt.

The miner stared at the kid, then flipped his cards face up and said, "Take it home," and the tunnel rat observed, "He was biting at you, son."

In the next hour, the kid won six hands, all of them big, yet Kalmikov couldn't decide whether the boy was just lucky or cheating. Looking down at his meager pile of chips, he decided to go for broke and let them fall where they would and the kid aced him out of the hand with three queens to his three jacks.

Staring at him, Kalmikov said softly, "Boy, I think you're cheating. They's only one way you get out of this room alive and that's to push in them stacks and get up and leave without looking back."

Still smiling, the boy's eyes suddenly turned wild and Kalmikov, wondering if he had made a bad mistake, nonetheless jerked his knife and with a wild shout, started over the table.

The kid was wearing two guns, one a .45 Colt at his right side, the other a .44 Russian top break in a holster that lay along his stomach, putting the butt of the pistol even with his belt buckle. It was this gun the kid drew and it came up and over the table top instantaneously, giving Kalmikov one brief glimpse of its gaping bore, then it roared twice and the big miner felt the terrible impact as the slugs bit deep, chewing their way through flesh and bone to burst out his back and shatter a mirror hanging behind him. As he was driven backwards, he lost his grip on the knife and then a great, black sheet settled over him and his last bitter thought was what a damn fool he had been.

The kid broke the gun, removed the two spent rounds, reloaded it from his belt, tossed the empties on the dead miner's chest, and gathered up his chips. Strolling to the bar he said, "Cash me in, bartender," and watched as the money was counted out in neat stacks in front of him. He did not look around, thus showing contempt for the possibility someone else might decide to even the score and put a bullet in his back. Stuffing the crisp bills in his coat pocket, he turned, surveyed the room with a smile, observed, "Feller can't always tell a horse by its color," in a soft Texas drawl and departed as quietly as he had come.

The shots that sent Big Al Kalmikov to Boot Hill carried plainly to the banks of the Green where Vent and Rose sat making plans. They were unaware of the fact that the object of their search was even now riding southwest along the Overland Trail toward the town of Green River nor that he had just carved yet another notch on his pistol butt.

Rising, Vent said, "Reckon we best go have a look around town and see if we can't turn up the boy," and they tramped through the sagebrush and down the alley where Vent suddenly hauled up and Rose, walking close behind, bumped into him.

A diminutive rider with prematurely grey hair had just led five men from a saloon half a block down the street and now he stopped and looked around and then headed for the livery on the north end of town.

"Hard-looking bunch, ain't they?" Vent observed.

"Them ain't no second raters, Vent," Rose said. "Them's the pick of the litter."

Vent was inclined to agree. Deciding this was no time for a confrontation, he led the way across the street and into the livery where they had left the horses, grateful to have chosen a stable other than the one being used by the Barbed-T. Vent knew the Appaloosa was a dead giveaway, but he wouldn't have traded him for the famous Denton mare everybody said Sam Bass won so much money with. The Appy suited Vent and the two had been through some hard times together and he had no doubt there would be other times in the future.

As they were saddling their horses, the liveryman, a talkative oldster, rattled away a mile a minute, then asked, "You boys hear the news? Bob Ford shot Jesse James two days ago . . . and now we just had us a shootin' right here in Rock Springs . . . some long-haired feller. Me, I'm guessing it was Wild Bill Hickok, filled Big Al Kalmikov full of lead over at the Sundance Saloon. Plugged him dead center twice, they said. Gent that saw it told me you could cover the holes with a playing card . . ."

Vent turned and looked at the old man and then said softly, "Describe this gent."

The liveryman looked at the floor, then up into Vent's eyes and said hastily, "Well, hell, I didn't see him myself, but this friend of mine, he said the feller was just a kid. Had curly gold hair, blue eyes that was cold as a block of Flaming Gorge ice, and was pretty enough to be mistook for a girl. He had on all black, they say and carried two big sixes . . ."

Vent looked at Rose and asked, "That him?"

Rose, his mouth a bitter line, said, "That's him. Let's ride," and Vent tossed the liveryman a dollar and they mounted and left town at a high lope.

Cap Stalls led his men from the livery on the north side of town and then pulled in at the marshal's office and dismounted, handed his reins to Whitey Beard, said, "Wait," and went in.

The marshal, a man who had obviously spent more time at the table than he did on a horse, glanced up over the toes of his boots, where they rested comfortably on top of his desk, and asked, "What can I do for you, friend?"

Stalls looked at the fat marshal sourly and said, "Looking for a feller by the name of Vent Torrey. Seen him around here?"

The marshal slowly removed his feet from his desk and eyes wide, asked, "Is he in my territory?"

"Hell, I don't know. That's what I'm trying to find out from you."

"Well, just who the hell are you?" the marshal asked belligerently.

Stalls was beginning to lose his temper. Staring at the man, he said distinctly, "I'm the superintendent of the Barbed-T Ranch over at South Pass. I work for Elam Jordan."

Even this far away, Elam Jordan's name was one to conjure up a vision of absolute power. That knowledge now showed on the marshal's face as he said, "Why didn't you say so? Hell, my name's Slate Carter. Anything I can do for you, just name her."

"I already did," Stalls said patiently.

Carter looked blank for a moment then said, "Oh yeah, Vent Torrey. Nope, ain't heard hide nor hair of him. Been some excitement around here today so I might just have missed out on spotting him."

"Excitement?"

The marshal grinned sourly and nodded. "Some kid over at the Sundance up and bored Al Kalmikov; put two slugs right smack dab through his ticker. Killed old Al as dead as a nit, he did."

Stalls stared at him. "Who the hell is Al Kalmikov?"

"Why hell, he's the foreman up at the Big Iron Mine. Everybody knows that."

"Well, I didn't know it," Stalls said disgustedly. "Who did the shooting?"

"Kid by the name of Rose," the marshal answered.

Stalls, in the act of taking out his tobacco, stopped his hand at his shirt pocket and asked quietly, "That wouldn't have been Carroll Rose, would it?"

"That's him, all right," Carter said. "Why? You know him?"

"Hell, Carter, just about everybody from here to California and here to east Texas knows that kid. He's put down a dozen men."

"He has?" the marshal asked and his face slowly turned white.

"Yep," then noting Carter's rapid paling, asked, "What's the matter, you go after him, did you?"

"I sure as hell did," Carter admitted. "Only he'd left town."

"Which way did he go?"

"Liveryman said he rode south," Carter told him.

Stalls nodded and turned to the door and then the marshal said, "By the way, they was two fellers stopped in here a week or so ago looking for Rose. One of them wore a real funny glove. Danged thing went clear up around his arm. They didn't hang around long . . . couple of grubliners, I reckon."

Stalls remained completely motionless for a long breath, then said mildly, "Thanks, Mr. Carter," and quietly left the office.

Accepting his reins from Beard, he said, "He's been here. Rode through about a week ago. Was with another gent . . . they was looking for Carroll Rose."

Beard stared at him. "Carroll Rose? Now what the hell you reckon the tie-up there is?"

Jeff Kidder said mildly, "I don't think I want to know. If Rose is a friend of Torrey's, we got problems a lot bigger than him."

"Yeah, and who the hell is the other gent with Leatherhand?" Hance Hall wondered.

"There's only one way to find out," Stalls said. "Let's go ask 'em."

Two weeks later, they rode into Kanab, Utah. Their horses were about done and the men looked as if they had been at the Battle of the Little Big Horn with Custer.

Looking over his beaten men, Stalls said, "Boys, this here town ain't much, but I reckon we best take a few days and lay up here. I'll wire the old man and let him know what's happening."

"Reckon that means you'll let him know about nothing," Powers observed with a grin.

"I'm beginning to figure just maybe Torrey knows we're on his trail," Stalls said.

"Hell, everywhere we been, he's been there just ahead of us, and just before him and that old man get there, the Rose kid's been and gone," Hall said. "What the hell we playing, follow the leader?"

"I can't rightly say," Stalls admitted, "but I'm gonna figure out a way we can get there first for once."

"If I don't find something to eat pretty soon, my stomach's gonna figure some varmint cut my throat without me even knowing it," Bright said.

After arranging for their horses, Stalls and his men went in search of a restaurant and discovered the town had only one eating place and that was in a saloon. Looking around, Stalls said, "Some town. A livery, a saddle shop, Wells Fargo, half a dozen houses, and a saloon."

The saloon was empty when Stalls and his men entered it and found a large table near the back. The bartender, a nondescript individual that would have been completely missed in a crowd, looked up from a six-week-old newspaper and, eyes bleary enough to match his red-veined nose, asked dispiritedly, "What'll you boys have?"

"What you got to eat?" Stalls asked.

"Got some stew. It'll put iron in yore blood and ink in your quill and the price is right," the bartender bragged.

"Never mind the damn price, just haul it out here and bring a bottle of whiskey with it . . . and make damn sure it ain't that Indian horse crap with the snake heads in it," Stalls ordered.

"Damn stuff's probably poison by the looks of that ranahan," Jeff Kidder said.

"Whiskey'll probably boil the lining outa a man's guts," Hance Hall growled.

"Damned feller sure don't seem to care about business," Roy Powers observed.

Bright, staring at the door to the kitchen, said, "Me, I don't give a damn what's in the stew or the whiskey. Right now I'd eat the north end of a skunk going south."

Whitey Beard said nothing as his cold eyes surveyed the room, noting a stairway leading to a second floor and a back door he figured let out into an alley.

Stalls, watching him, asked, "Reading the place?"

"Feller should," Beard said.

Then the kitchen door swung wide and a woman came through carrying a large tray and the men's head swiveled as if they were all on the same string. She was tall, wide-hipped and big busted, and had blonde hair down to her waist. Her face was classically beautiful, each line exactly where it should be. Small ears framed wide blue eyes and a pert nose set off a pair of full lips.

"Jesus!" Bright exclaimed, his empty belly forgotten.

"Lord, Lord," Powers mumbled.

"As I live and breathe," Hall said.

Jeff Kidder stared speechless and even Beard, a man of monumentally cold nerves, found himself staring, as did Stalls.

"Welcome to Kanab, gentlemen," the woman said as she set the tray down on the table. Hands on hips, she looked them over, allowing her eyes to linger on Stalls the longest, then said, "I'm Helga Peterson and I own the Montezuma Inn," and she leaned over and every eye fastened on the drooping front of her blouse as the Barbed-T riders held their breath and prayed silently that the low-cut affair would sag yet another inch.

Placing the plates in front of each man, and seemingly unaware of their spellbound stares, she straightened up to sighs all around and said, "I'll go fetch the bread and the coffee," and turned and walked to the kitchen.

As she made her way to the bar, Beard, who had never been known to comment on any woman before, said reverently, "Me, I'm gonna move to this town and stay here forever."

"You're gonna have company then," Powers warned him.

"Hell boys, a woman like that, she's enough for the whole damned Barbed-T crew," Hance Hall observed.

Eyes following the woman through the kitchen door, Kidder mused, "Wonder if we could talk her into coming back to the ranch as a mascot?"

When she returned with bread and coffee, Stalls asked, "Ma'am, we're looking for a couple of friends of ours that may have passed this way . . . A tall young feller name of Torrey and an older man."

She smiled and it was devastating. "Why yes, they were here two days ago. Seems they were looking for a young man named Carroll Rose."

"Did they find him?" Stalls asked.

"I reckon they just didn't look hard enough," a voice said. Turning, the men saw a young man with long curly gold hair and smiling blue eyes standing at the bar, a grin on his face.

"Carroll Rose," Beard said softly.

The woman went over to him and kissed him quickly, and smiling over her shoulder impishly, went back to the kitchen, passing the sour-faced bartender and patting him on the cheek, to which he showed not one iota of emotion or reaction, but continued to lean on the plank reading his six-week-old paper.

" 'Lo, Whitey," Rose said. "Been awhile . . ."

"Yep, reckon it has," Beard agreed.

"Heard you boys was looking for Leatherhand. That right?"

Stalls nodded. "Elam Jordan wants to talk to him."

"More like hang him," Rose said, still smiling.

"Nope, just wants to hear his side of a two-sided story," Stalls replied.

"Well, I'm gonna tell you boys something," Rose declared. "That old man traveling with Vent Torrey happens to be my paw. If he has an accident, like getting in the way of some stray lead, I'd just naturally take it unkindly."

Bright looked at Stalls and back at Rose and said, "Mister, you talk a hell of a fight, but they's six of us here. If we take a notion to put you down, I reckon you best go make the arrangements."

Rose continued to smile, but Stalls, watching him, saw a subtle change take place on his face and suddenly felt the cold wind of death pass through that room and thought inanely, damn, and I haven't even eaten yet.

Looking at Stalls, Rose asked, "Who's the mouthy feller?"

"What the hell you wanta know for?" Bright demanded and Stalls thought of the number of men he had watched dig their own graves with their mouths and wondered when the notoriously unpredictable Rose would start shooting.

Rose looked off over Bright's head and said softly, "I kinda like to know the names of the fellers I'm about to send off on the long ride . . . ."

As Rose spoke, Stalls felt the hair on the back of his neck begin to tingle and thought, he's insane, and wondered why nobody had ever mentioned it before.

Bright, suddenly becoming aware of just how close he was to dying, and realizing this wasn't a man you could scare with six men or the whole damn crew of the Barbed-T, said sullenly, "Name's Bright and I'm the damn fool who's been letting his mouth overload his butt."

The panther retreated from Rose's eyes as he said, "Sometimes a man's pride gets in the way," and turned his back on the Barbed-T crew and said, "Jack, fetch me a whiskey, will you, old son?"

Wordlessly, the bartender poured Rose a drink and went back to his paper. Observing this, Stalls asked, "What's the matter with that feller?"

The bartender ignored the question.

Rose, still smiling, said, "Oh, he's married to Helga. Makes life kinda hard sometimes, living with a lady that every man within 500 miles wants. Can turn a feller plumb sour on life."

Powers shook his head and observed, "Hell, it'd be worth it."

Stalls, tired of the game, said, "Let's eat," and then looking up at Rose, invited, "You're welcome to join us."

"Thanks, but I promised Helga I'd help her hang some curtains upstairs," and he tossed off his whiskey and went to the second floor.

Shaking his head, Stalls bent to his meal.

Chapter Four

Grafton, Utah was a quiet Mormon town squatting in lonesome isolation on the banks of the Virgin River. It was surrounded by red rock cliffs and barren land that stretched in all directions, with the exception of about 200 acres along the river where water had turned things green and where the settlers had planted fields of vegetables.

As Vent and Denton Rose walked their tired horses along Main Street, they checked each alley and building, but the town was as quiet as its graveyard to the southeast of town beside the road from Kanab and Arizona.

They had been informed by a marshal at Bloomington that mention was made there by somebody who met Carroll Rose.

Said the marshal, "He put a feller down in Rock Springs, then I hear tell he floated in and out of half a dozen places. Now he's supposed to be in Grafton, but that there's a Mormon town. Nothin' much gone on there and damn certain no gambling."

Vent had thanked the man and now he and Rose were riding into the quiet little town, with its handsome church and scatter of buildings. There was no saloon, but a mercantile store squatted halfway along the street, and it was here the two men pulled up to allow their horses to drink from an overflowing water trough.

As they sat looking around, a tall man riding a Claybank gelding suddenly appeared from behind a building down street and came on. He was dressed in range garb and Vent saw sunlight flash from a full shellbelt as the man approached.

When he arrived at the mercantile, he reined his horse over and, nodding at Vent and Rose, stepped down, tossed the reins over a hitching post, and went inside.

"Gent looks familiar," Rose said.

"He's got a lot of hard bark on him," Vent observed and, reining over to the hitchrack, stepped down and left the Appaloosa ground tied. Rose dismounted and they walked through the wide door of the store. Its dimly lit interior was a mad jumble of everything a man could want to ranch, farm, or hunt. The tall man was standing, leaning against the counter, eating a can of peaches. He did not look up.

The mercantile owner turned and nodded as Vent walked to the counter and Rose began gathering the grub they needed.

Leaning on the counter, Vent asked, "You got any .44 shells?"

"Yes sir, I do," the man said and went and fetched a box and placed them on the counter, then observed, "You fellers' horses look like they could use a rest and some good grain."

Vent smiled. "They've come aways," he agreed.

The tall man pulled back his coat and Vent saw he was wearing a brace of .45 Colt frontier model double-actions. These guns had first begun appearing in stores four years earlier and Vent had once tried one and found he didn't care for the balance.

Nodding at Vent's gun, the stranger observed, "That's a pretty old .44 you got there. Mind if I look at it?"

Vent glanced at him and shook his head. "No offense meant, friend, but I never let my gun outa my hands. Sorta habit I got. Figure it's a good way to stay alive."

The man grinned, and looking at Vent's leather-covered right hand, observed softly, "From what I hear, Mr. Torrey, they's a lot of men who met up with you and kept their guns and still died."

Rose turned then and stood watching as Vent said, "You have me at a disadvantage, sir."

"I'm Tom Horn of Arizona," the man said. He didn't offer to shake hands and, after hearing his name, Vent wasn't expecting it.

"You've kinda left a trail behind you, too, Mr. Horn," Vent said.

Horn smiled. "Only rustlers and hostiles," and he went back to spooning up peaches.

The store owner, suddenly confronted by two customers who were famed all over the west for killing other men, looked at Vent nervously and asked, "You fellers need anything else?"

Rose gathered up the food he had put aside and came to the counter. Pointing to a large cured ham hanging from a string, he said, "We'll take that ham. Is it heavy salt or light?"

Reaching up and untying the string, the store owner replied, "It's salted, but the feller who cures these don't overdo it. You can eat this here ham in the middle of the desert and never get thirsty."

Horn sat the empty can on the counter, nodded at the store owner, and turned and walked to the door, then, looking across his shoulder, said, "You boys ever get to Cheyenne, look me up. I'll buy you a drink," and he was gone.

They heard the sound of his horse's hooves pounding north out of town as they left the store and Vent looked at Rose and said, "Now I wonder what that gent's doing in a town like Grafton?"

"I don't know," Rose replied, "but I do know he's planted a lot of people and from what they say, most of them died without ever seeing his face."

"Reckon some fellers don't believe in taking chances," Vent observed and mounted the Appaloosa.

The next day they rode into Silver Reef and found a town that was living on the back side of a boom. Vent figured it wouldn't be long before it was only a memory.

He had heard that the mines there gave up $8 million a year in silver bullion, but that the take had tapered off to a mere trickle now and the boomers were moving on. As they rode down the main stem, with its boardwalks reaching over a mile on both sides of the street, the lack of pedestrian traffic was a dead giveaway. Here was a town that had howled at the moon until its voice grew hoarse and was now sitting back on its haunches with its tongue hanging out.

Rose glanced at Vent and asked, "Food or drink?"

They were just passing one of the town's many saloons so Vent turned in and, stepping down, loosened his cinch and left the horse ground tied. They tramped into the low, stone building and found it was almost cold inside.

Sitting at a back table with a bottle and glasses, Vent could feel himself unwind as he relaxed in the glow of good liquor. In the days past, he had learned a lot about Rose. You couldn't help but discern a man's pedigree if you rode with him long enough, Vent knew, and he had found the older man intelligent, methodical, loyal to his friends, and a bad enemy. By listening to stories Rose told about his ranch and the people of east Texas, he also learned the ex-rancher was a man with a better than average education, having attended a university at Fort Worth for a year after completing the lower grades. He had read extensively and even now carried several thin volumes in his saddlebags. Often at night, when Vent had rolled up in his blankets, Rose would sit and read by the dim light of the campfire.

When it came to talking about his son, Rose would become animated, describing how smart the boy was and the things he did when but a child. Vent hoped fervently the ex-rancher wouldn't find a mudhole at the end of the rainbow they were chasing. From what he had heard about Carroll Rose, Vent guessed the man was beyond helping. He had left too many men lying in the dust of the street, or face down in some two-by-four bustout joint, to ride away and forget it all. He was marked just as surely as if someone had put a branding iron to his forehead and tallied him a shootist. Vent knew he would never find a safe haven where he could settle down, and he was sure young Rose wouldn't either. There was a line a man crossed when he went to the gun that he could never step back over. It was there as surely as if someone had painted it in the dust. Vent knew it and he was beginning to think that just maybe Rose knew it.

Looking at the older man, Vent thought, hell, a man's gotta try, and downed his whiskey and said, "Shall we go put on the feed bag?"

They returned the bottle to the bartender, paid for the drinks, and walked out the front door into a gun trap.

As Vent hit the sidewalk, he looked up and stopped. Six men stood in a semi-circle in the middle of the street facing him. Rose, who had stepped to the left when he saw the men, said quietly, "Meet the Barbed-T."

Vent had his look and figured if it came to a shooting, he would go down. Suddenly stubborn, he made a decision then not to go with this bunch even if he died for it.

And so he marked an invisible line behind him and vowed silently he'd not cross it, and flipped the tiedown from his gun hammer and waited.

Cap Stalls stepped out in front of his men and said quietly, "You can't win, Mr. Torrey. You know that, don't you?"

Vent smiled. "Mr. Stalls, that ain't gonna mean a damn thing to you because I'm going to put lead in you first," and he pointed to Beard with a thumb and said, "Whitey there, he'll be next and I think I might even manage to put away your Injun while I'm at it."

Glancing at Rose, Stalls said, "Mr. Rose, this ain't your tango. You can sit this one out."

Rose shook his head. "Mr. Stalls, I think I'll hang around and see what kind of music you play."

Stalls looked at the ground, then up into Vent's eyes and said, "Mr. Jordan, he didn't tell us to kill you, Mr. Torrey. He just said to bring you to the Barbed-T so he could hear your side of the story."

"And if he happens to be feeling ornery that day, he'll just sorta have me hanged to brighten his day, huh?"

"Elam Jordan is a fair man," Stalls said stiffly.

"If you wanta know what happened in that saloon, you ask Hep Alkire," Vent counseled. "He won't lie to you . . . or you could ask that wet-eared pup you got with you. He was there."

Bright stepped forward and, dropping his hand to his gun, snapped, "Who the hell you calling a wet-ear?"

Vent's face suddenly turned bleak and cold as he looked

at Bright. "Take your hand off that gun, you son-of-a-bitch, or you're dead meat."

Bright jerked his hand away from his pistol and, looking at Stalls, asked plaintively, "You gonna let him get away with calling me that?"

Stalls stared at him. "Dammit, Bobby, that's between you and him."

Bright stood mute.

Ignoring him then, Vent looked at Stalls and said quietly, "Mr. Stalls, you're wasting your time. I ain't going anywhere with you. You go back and tell Elam Jordan if he wants to talk to me, why he can just straddle a horse and name the neutral ground and I'll be there."

Stalls shook his head stubbornly, "That ain't my orders, Mr. Torrey."

"You ready to die for your orders?" Vent asked, looking curiously at the Barbed-T segundo.

"If need be," Stalls replied.

"In that case, Mr. Stalls, turn your wolves loose whenever you're a mind to and I'll see you in hell," Vent said bleakly.

Watching him, Vent knew Stalls was going to try it and he thought, he's a damn fool and so am I, then a cold voice cut across the tension of the street like the blade of an Indian's knife: "Mr. Stalls, you and your boys stand fast. If anybody goes to the gun in this town, he's undertaker bait."

Vent looked past the Barbed-T crew and a man with a star stood in the entrance to an alley holding a sawed-off Greener against his leg, his eyes flat and implacable as he watched Stalls and his men narrowly.

Stalls turned his head, took in the man and the shotgun, then a second man stepped out of a door on Vent's side of the street and stood on the sidewalk facing the Barbed-T crew. He also held a deadly sawed-off shotgun against his hip.

Vent smiled and said, " 'Lo there, Boots. How you makin' her?''

Boots Thomas grinned back and nodding his head at the man across the street, invited, "Meet my deputy, Crane Hardwell,'' and at the name, the Barbed-T crew suddenly ceased all movement. They had heard about this quiet man from Oklahoma whose penchant for using a shotgun had made him one of the most feared lawmen in the west. He had served in the Indian Nations under Heck Thomas as one of Judge Isaac Charles Parker of Fort Smith's deputies, and it was said had killed no less than twenty-six men in the line of duty.

Stalls looked at Vent and said, "Whipsawed. . . . Another time,'' and turned and led his men along the street to the livery. Ten minutes later they rode out of Silver Reef.

Vent walked across the street and shook hands with Thomas, noting, "Seems our trails keep crossing, Boots. When'd you leave Jerome?''

Vent had first worked as a deputy marshal for Thomas in Leadville, Colorado and later the lawman, working as chief marshal at the boom town of Jerome, Arizona, sided Vent in a fight against a large rancher who not only wanted Vent hanged, but also wanted half of Arizona under his brand. He accomplished neither.

As Hardwell strolled up, Thomas said, "Town got too tame for me. Ore started playing out and I figured she was heading for a ghost so I rode out. Took this job a year ago,'' and, glancing at Hardwell, said, "meet my deputy marshal. This here's Crane Hardwell. Crane, Vent Torrey. He used to work for me in Leadville.''

"Heard of you, Mister Torrey," Hardwell said.

Vent grinned. "You haven't passed notice around the country either, Mr. Hardwell."

"They's a damn good saloon up the street," Thomas informed them. "I'll buy you boys a drink."

Nodding at Rose, Vent said, "Meet Denton Rose of Texas," and watched the two lawmen's faces tighten as Thomas asked quietly, "Maybe it's none of my business, Mr. Rose, but as a lawman, I got to ask: You any kin to Carroll Rose?"

Looking squarely into Thomas' eyes, Rose said just as quietly, "Yes sir. He's my son."

Vent jerked his head toward the saloon and asked, "They got food down there?"

"Yes, they have," Thomas answered, still looking at Rose.

"Then let's go get her, Boots, and while we're eating, I'll fill you in on what that was all about out there in the street . . . and if Mr. Rose is a mind to, he can talk about his boy."

Elam Jordan stood before the big fireplace and stared at the telegram. Then he gazed out the window and began to wonder about this man Vent Torrey. It seemed that everywhere he went he found friends. Elam Jordan knew the West and he knew the men who lived there. They did not make friends with outlaws unless they too were outlaws. The code they lived by was a simple one. You kept your word and Elam Jordan himself had bought a thousand head of beef on a handshake and sold 200 horses on the same handshake. A man was loyal to his brand as long as the brand was straight. He did not mistreat good women and a man who beat up even a bad woman could find himself taking a quick trip to Boot Hill. The code insisted every man was responsible for his own debts and a debt unpaid was a debt owing and sooner or later it had to be made good. Decent men didn't mishandle horses and more than one fight had erupted in cow camps over some brute beating a horse.

Elam Jordan knew all this. He also knew that Hep Alkire's word was good and that if a man traveled with a gent like Denton Rose, he had to have some redeeming qualities. Jordan knew who Rose was. He had an excellent reputation in east Texas, where Jordan had bought more than one herd of cows.

Walking to the liquor cabinet, Jordan poured himself a glass half full of whiskey and, moving back to the window, thought about the telegram.

Boots Thomas was an honest lawman and was known from Colorado to Arizona. Now, according to Cap Stalls' telegram, he and that Oklahoma gunfighter, Crane Hardwell, had sided this Leatherhand.

Worse yet, Rose's son had braced Stalls and his men and warned them away from Denton Rose. The maniacal, baby-faced killer didn't seem concerned over Vent Torrey's fate; his only worry was for his father. And Denton Rose was riding with Torrey.

And suddenly Elam Jordan knew that Bitters, Kid Calamity, and Bobby Bright had flat-out lied to him. Walking to the front door, he called in a rider who had been sitting on the bunkhouse steps mending a pair of chaps and sent him to bring Bitters and the Kid in from the line shack they had been ordered to hold down.

Vent and Rose rode out of Silver Reef two days after the confrontation with the Barbed-T crew. Thomas had listened to Denton Rose's story and then told him word had filtered into Silver Reef that the young gunfighter was heading for Nevada. Vent knew the gold camps in that state would be a big attraction for a man who made his living gambling, so he and the ex-rancher turned their horses' heads west and three days later skirted the Escalante desert to the south, stopped long enough in Enterprise to buy more grub, then pushed on to Uvada, a stage stop on the Nevada border.

As they rode into the yard, the rattle of harness chains and the cracking sound of thoroughbraces hard driven against the body of a Concord coach, signaled the arrival of the Overland Stage.

"Haaaa . . . You ornery, slab-sided sons-a-bitches, git up there," the man on the box shouted as the six-up slammed into and out of a dip just east of the stage stop. Then the driver was hauling the coach to a gravel, dust-heaving stop at the door of the station and, as the convey-ance sat rocking gently, he dropped to the ground and opened the door, stepping aside to allow his passengers to escape for a few minutes.

The shotgun guard looked narrowly at Vent and Rose, carefully taking in their low-hung guns, scabbard rifles, and top-grade horses and figured them for either lawmen or outlaws.

Watching him drop to the ground, Vent thought, he's carrying bullion on that stage and it's made him nervous, and rode to the water trough where he and Rose allowed their horses to drink.

As the relief team was brought up, a man came from the station and called, "Hey, you fellers, that water will cost you half a dollar a horse."

Vent lifted the Appy's head and rode to where the man was standing and asked, "Where's the water come from, friend?"

The station operator had his look at this tall, quiet man, noting the strange glove on his right hand and the bottomless brown eyes that seemed to look holes through him and decided the price of water had just dropped.

"Windmill pumps it up from a well," he said as Rose rode over, hooked a leg around the saddle horn, and slowly rolled a cigarette.

"Shallow well, is it?" Vent asked as Rose scratched a match on his thumb and lit his cigarette.

"Hell no," the station manager replied. "It's a good producing well. Ain't no way it'll ever run dry."

"How long ago did you dig it?" Vent asked, still staring at the man.

"Didn't. Injuns dug it. We just put up the windmill."

"When was that?" Vent inquired, and his voice was soft and almost uncaring.

"Why, I reckon it must have been seven years ago or better," the man answered, not understanding what this tall man was reaching for.

Vent glanced at Rose and said, "Looks to me like this here feller has paid for that windmill half a dozen times over," then he looked back at the station manager and asked, "What's your name?"

"Why, it's Tatum. William Tatum. I run this here place . . ."

Vent looked him over carefully, noting the ragged condition of his clothes and the battered hat he wore. His hip was gunless and he wasn't wearing a coat, so Vent figured he didn't have a hideout gun.

"What you got in the way of food?" he asked.

"Got stew; got deer and beef steaks; got eggs and we even got us some vegetables. Squaw plants a garden every year . . ."

"Any whiskey?" Rose asked.

The station manager grinned. "Yes sir, we got some of the best damn sour mash you ever wrapped your lip around."

Vent nodded. "We'll try your stew and your whiskey, then we'll pay you for what we get, but I feel bound to tell you, Mr. Tatum, that I don't hold with a man profiteering off folks' need for water—not in this country."

"Hell, mister, forget the water," Tatum said magnanimously. "If a feller trades in my store, then he gets the water free. I thought maybe you boys was just passing through."

"Kind of you," Vent said drily and rode to the hitch rack, dismounted and loosened his cinch as Rose followed suit. As they entered the station, the driver came out, and poking his head back through the door, shouted, "Time to roll, folks. You got five minutes," and went to the coach and began checking harness.

The inside of the station was thirty degrees cooler than it was outside. Vent found it a welcome relief after the heat of the Escalante. Even though it was still spring, the desert could be a rough place to travel during the day. At night it dropped enough degrees to force a man into his coat.

They ate the stew and found it surprisingly good, then ordered a bottle, drank two drinks, and paid for the meal and the whiskey and, grinning, Vent tossed the man a silver cartwheel, observing, "I reckon a man's got to bring in a reasonable profit, Mr. Tatum, and I figure the money you make off that well probably goes in your pocket and not the company's."

Tatum grinned sheepishly, then nodded. "I get fifty dollars a month and food from them. It don't leave much to do with and I got five kids."

"Then you're welcome to it," Vent told him and stepped onto the porch and stood watching the stage pull away. A moment before the driver cracked his sixteen-foot bull whip, Vent caught a glimpse of several men riding into a low swell north of the station and recognized Whitey

Beard and Stalls. Then the boiling dust from the stage
obscured them and Vent leaped off the steps and quickly
led the horses around behind the building and turned them
into a small shed there. Tightening the cinches, he pulled
rifles from scabbards and entered the back door just as
Rose started out the front.

"Denton," Vent called sharply and something in the
Missourian's voice stopped Rose just inside the door.

"We got company," Vent said and Rose came back
into the room. Tossing him the Winchester, Vent glanced
at Tatum and asked sharply, "You got family in this
building, Mr. Tatum?"

Tatum shook his head. "Gone to Gunlock to visit
relatives. What the hell's going on here? You boys wanted?"

Vent grinned. "Not by the law, we ain't. We got a
problem with some fellers from over the other side of the
divide . . ."

"Where they at?" Rose asked.

"Just north of the station, and they know we're here.
They saw the Appy," Vent said sourly.

"The horses still out there?" Rose asked.

"I took them around back," Vent said, then glancing at
Tatum, jerked a thumb toward the back door and advised,
"You best light a shuck outa here, Mr. Tatum. These boys
can get right het up. They might just figure to plug you
too, if they get the idea you're sheltering us."

Tatum shook his head. "This here's an Overland Stage
station. Ain't no man gonna run me outa here. Hell, if I
taken off the company'd up and fire me," and he walked
behind the counter and came back carrying a rifle, a box of
shells and a handgun in a shell belt. As he strapped the
pistol on, he looked at Vent and asked, "You fellers mind
tellin' me who the hell I'm fixing to croak with?"

Glancing at Rose, Vent observed, "This here's one

optimistic feller," then as Tatum punched shells into the rifle, told him, "I'm Vent Torrey from Missouri and this gent's Denton Rose of east Texas."

Tatum stopped feeding shells into the rifle and looked up at Vent. "Leatherhand, by God," he said.

"Some folks call me that," Vent agreed.

"Them fellers out there must be crazy to jump you," Tatum observed.

"They's six of them," Vent informed him drily.

"Oh . . . Well, they got their work cut out for 'em if they figure to shoot their way in here. This place was made to stand off a whole war party of Injuns and has, more'n once. Let the bastards come," and he walked to the front windows and began closing heavy wooden shutters.

"Vent Torrey," a voice called. Vent looked at Rose and grinned.

It was Stalls and now he shouted again. "Either you come out, or we come in and get you. Either way, you're going back to South Pass City."

"They anyplace to shoot from upstairs?" Vent asked, and Tatum nodded as a sudden roar of gunfire cut off the words he was about to speak and sent him in a dive to the floor.

As bullets chunked into the front of the station, Vent sat calmly at a table in the middle of the room removing shells from their boxes and dropping them into his chap pockets.

"Mr. Tatum," he called. When the station keeper twisted his head around to stare at Vent, the gunfighter said, "I'm keeping track of these here shells. When this is over, I'll pay for them."

"And I'll take it if I'm still alive," Tatum answered, then ducked again as another fusilage struck the building. This time several slugs ploughed between the logs, drilling into pots and pans hanging behind the store counter and blasting several whiskey bottles into shattered glass.

"Goddamn those highbinders," Tatum shouted, but he remained on the floor.

Picking up his rifle, Vent walked to the stairs and, looking back at Rose, said, "Watch that back door in case they try a fox run," and Rose nodded as Vent took the stairs two at a time.

A catwalk ran around three sides of the second floor, giving Vent a clear view down inside the store and bar. Doors let off from the catwalk and Vent figured this was where Tatum and his family lived. Some of the rooms were probably for rent if a man took a notion he wanted to stay over a night to rest sore bones, butts, and backs after riding too many miles in one of the Concords, which Vent always figured had an evil capacity to hit every bump on the road. He catwalked along the upper floor until he came to the front of the building, then let himself into one of the bedrooms and found window glass all over the bed and floor. One of Stalls' men had used the window for target practice. Looking at it, Vent thought, saves me the trouble of kicking it out and knelt on the edge of the bed, had his look, and saw a man squatted behind a wood pile. Lifting the 38.40, he dropped the sights on the man's chest, started to take up the slack, then deliberately held to the right and shot the gunman in the left shoulder, spinning him away into open ground, where he lay clutching his shoulder and staring up at the window as if expecting a killing shot. Instead, Vent hit the floor as a storm of lead hammered at the frame and poured into the room, turning the door and the inside wall into a pockmarked series of deep gouges.

Looking at it, Vent mumbled, "More holes than Aunt Maude's flour sifter," and moved to another window.

Removing his hat, he carefully peeped around the sill and spotted yet another Barbed-T rider. This one was standing at the door of the horse barn reloading his rifle. Deliberately Vent shot him through the legs and watched as the big slug kicked them out from under him and dropped him on his face in the dust. Again Vent moved and more lead showered the room. Crawling to the shattered door, he ran along the upper deck, glancing down as he stood up, and trotted to a room facing north and ducked inside. He had noted that both Tatum and Rose were firing through slits in the shutters and wondered if they had hit anyone.

This time as he peered out, he saw no one and decided they had had their lesson and wouldn't make that mistake again. Rising, he walked back downstairs, and Rose and Tatum ceased firing and turned and looked at Vent as he asked, "Where you keep your water, Mr. Tatum?"

"In the kitchen, but they ain't much. Just a five-gallon bucket is all."

Looking at the rows of whiskey bottles, Vent shook his head, then observed, "Well, if it runs out, we can always drink whiskey. That way if them old boys out there manage to take us down, we won't give a damn."

Both defenders grinned at Vent, then ducked as a new volley slammed into the house.

"Persistent bastards, ain't they?" Rose observed.

"Reckon we best save our ammo and just wait," Vent counseled.

"Hell, I got ten thousand rounds back there," Tatum said.

Vent looked at Tatum and smiled. "Mr. Tatum, I'm a frugal man. Don't believe in waste. Mother Torrey, she always said, 'Waste not, want not' and I kinda figure that's good advice. Besides, I promised I'd pay for the ammo and at the rate you fellers are going, I'll have to work for the Overland for the next twenty years to fetch myself outa debt.''

So they sat on the floor and played cards and waited.

Elam Jordan shouted, ''Come in,'' and watched Bitters and Kid Calamity straggle into the room. The Kid still had a bandage on his wounded hand and Bitters' arm was in a sling.

Pointing to a couch, Jordan said, ''Sit down,'' and walked over and leaned against the rough stone of the fireplace. As he stared at the two men, they refused to meet his eyes, but instead looked at the floor or at something on the far wall.

''You know, boys, they's one thing I won't tolerate and that's a lying man,'' he said, his gimlet eyes still fastened on the men.

''Hell, who said we lied?'' Bitters asked.

''Everything I've found out about this gent Torrey shows me you boys lied,'' and when The Kid would have spoken, Jordan held up an imperious hand and said, ''I had Hep bring me every man jack that was in that saloon and every damn one of them said you, Mr. Bitters, deliberately tripped Jake and it wasn't the first time you pulled something like that. You're a bully Mr. Bitters, and you, Kid, you're a fool to put yourself in harness with this idiot.''

The Kid looked uncomfortable, then said defensively, ''Hell, Mr. Jordan, I couldn't just sit by and let that drifter pound old Tag's head in with his pistol.''

''You couldn't, huh? Well, Kid, you should have because I'm gonna fire Mr. Bitters and you can go along with him and keep him out of trouble the next time he pulls some stunt, and believe me, Kid, he will.''

The Kid looked blank. ''You mean you're firing us?''

"Go to the head of the class, sonny," Jordan said drily.

When both of them would have spoken at once Jordan held up his hand and pointed at the door. "I want you boys off Barbed-T land before the sun goes down. If you're found here after that, I've given orders to the rest of the men to shoot you on sight."

Bitters looked at The Kid and said, "Come on. We know when we're not wanted. They's other outfits in Wyoming Territory."

"Not for you two, they ain't," Jordan told them. "I've put out the word. You're blackballed. No ranch in this part of the country will hire you. . . . Now git!"

They got.

The next day Jordan was leaning against the breaking corral watching one of his bronc twisters top off a bucker when a Barbed-T rider came in at a gallop. Pulling the horse up at the corral, he nodded at Jordan, who looked at the blown horse and said, "Pete, you best have a damn good reason for riding that horse down," and waited.

The rider dug a folded telegram from his pocket and said, "This here just came in. Thought you'd want to see it."

Jordan took the yellow sheet and nodding at the man's horse, said, "Walk him around. Good rub down. Slow watering. You know what to do. Do it."

When the rider was gone, Jordan leaned against the fence and read the telegram and a frown crossed his face. Turning to where one of his men was just saddling up to go out on the range, he shouted, "Elbert, saddle me a horse and go over to the bunkhouse and get Mick O'Reilly," and he spun on his heel and headed for the house.

When he came out, he was wearing a mackinaw and a shell belt with twin .45s in cutaway holsters. Walking to the barn, he accepted the reins from the rider called Elbert and wordlessly led him and Mick O'Reilly toward South Pass City.

Mick O'Reilly, a taciturn Irishman who was said to be Jordan's personal gunfighter, was well known in Wyoming Territory. He was fast and had notched his gun more than once, but like a lot of men in his day, was a stranger to the rest of the country simply because he never left his home ground. He had been born at a mountain ranch near South Pass City before it was more than a stopover for immigrants and had worked for Elam Jordan for years. Although the rest of the Barbed-T crew was unaware of it, O'Reilly drew down as much money as did Stalls, for his was a unique position on the ranch. Jordan used him to solve problems. When nesters began moving in on the big ranch, it was O'Reilly who persuaded them they should go someplace else, pointing out that the country just wasn't suited to farming. He had patiently explained that others who had come had almost starved when crops failed to grow in the rocky soil and were forced to live off Barbed-T beef.

"When this happened we hanged them," O'Reilly had said. The nesters got the message. They left.

From time to time O'Reilly performed other services for Jordan. Once, when a man reneged on a debt, Jordan sent O'Reilly to collect either the money or the man's dead body. The man said he didn't have any money, and even then O'Reilly might have given him a chance to get it, but when the debtor tried to trade his thirteen-year-old daughter as settlement, O'Reilly killed him.

Now he flanked Jordan as they rode into the main street of South Pass City and headed for the telegraph office. Hep Alkire was standing in front of the marshal's office and, when Jordan saw him, he turned in and sitting his horse ramrod straight, said, "Looks like you were right about Bitters and The Kid. I fired them."

"What about Bobby Bright?" Alkire asked.

"I'm on my way to the telegraph office. Gonna wire Stalls and tell him to get rid of Bright and come home . . . only they's a problem . . ."

Alkire walked to the edge of the sidewalk and leaning on a porch support, squinted up at Jordan and waited.

"Seems Stalls and my boys got Vent Torrey and a feller named Denton Rose trapped at the Uvada Stage Station. Torrey's done put two of them out of action."

Hep grinned. "Looks like it's a question of who's got who pinned down . . ."

"He's done shot Powers through the shoulder and broke both of Hance Hall's legs," Jordan said bitterly.

Alkire looked puzzled. "Old Vent must be gettin' downright charitable in his advancing years. Was a time when you'd have had two dead men to bury. Must be he ain't out to kill anybody."

Jordan nodded agreement. "That's what I figure, although I wouldn't blame him if he bumped them all off."

"Did you say Denton Rose was with him?" Alkire suddenly asked, his eyes narrowing.

"I did," Jordan replied.

"Well, you may not have to worry about Torrey putting your boys in the ground. Denton Rose's son is Carroll Rose and he's a out-and-out killer."

Jordan dug out the makings and put together a cigarette and, as he lit it, observed, "I know Carroll Rose and I know what can happen here if he takes a hand. Reckon I've made a damn fool mistake."

Alkire looked Jordan in the eye and said softly, "I can't disagree with that, Elam. They's another thing you best consider . . ."

Jordan waited, the smoke from his cigarette trickling up past his face, his eyes bleak.

"Leatherhand's the kinda gent that demands an accounting," Alkire said quietly. "He'll come for you, Elam. What I don't know and neither will you, is whether he'll come gunning or talkin'."

"Reckon I'll just have to deal with that when the time comes," Jordan avowed.

"I been through Uvada. That's a long ways from anywhere. How'd Stalls get a telegram to you?"

"He sent Jeff Kidder to Pioche. He's waiting there for my answer," Jordan replied.

Alkire stared at him. "You mean Stalls sent Kidder away and he's got two men down? Hell, by the time Kidder gets back, he may be the only man left."

"Whitey Beard's with Stalls," Jordan said.

Alkire looked down street and shook his head. "Beard's good, Elam, but he's a long day's ride from being in Vent Torrey's class. Hell, man, Torrey's downed the best. You know how many men he's killed?"

"I heard he lost count," Jordan said drily.

"He don't notch his gun, if that's what you're saying," Alkire grinned, "but men who know him say his dead count is between twenty-five and thirty men."

Jordan glanced at O'Reilly and O'Reilly, his face as still as a Mississippi River gambler's pushing for a five-thousand-dollar pot, shrugged.

"Reckon I best send that telegram," Jordan said, then turned back and looking at Alkire, told him, "I fired Bitters and The Kid. I'm going to order Stalls to get rid of Bobby Bright and come home. Best I can do," and rode down street, turning in at the telegraph office.

Five minutes later he came out and mounted his horse and rode to the bank, stepped down and, handing his reins to Elbert, went in. When he re-emerged, he held a sheaf of bills in his hand. Mounting again he led his men to the train depot and handing O'Reilly the money, said, "Go to Uvada," then glancing at Elbert, tossed him a silver dollar and ordered, "Get a drink, Elbert. I'll pick you up on the way out," and waited until he was gone, then continued, "When you get out there, put a bullet in Bright. Then stick to this feller Torrey. I got me a hunch Bitters and that kid will try for him. I want both of them dead."

Putting the money in his coat pocket, O'Reilly dismounted, handed the reins to Jordan, said, "See you," and walked into the depot.

Jordan turned his horse and rode back up town, wondering about a man who would take on an assignment to kill three fellers and not say a damn word.

Tag Bitters slouched deep in his saddle as the rain pounded down, sagging the brim of his hat and running into his clothes. He was wet, miserable, and mad. Glancing at The Kid, he wondered how the hell he'd got tangled up with the flash gunman in the first place. But then, he ruefully admitted the reason he traveled with such men as The Kid and Bobby Bright was because other, better men shunned him and his company. He did not know why and had never tried to find out. At thirty-four, he had worked for eleven outfits, had gone up the trail on drives twice, and had been shot three times. He knew he was no match for a man good with a gun. Hell knows, he'd practiced. Hadn't he spent hours on end drawing and firing his .45, spending half his wages for shells, to no avail? He was still slow and always would be. The Kid, on the other hand, was faster than some, but Bitters knew his pedigree. He was a man who'd shoot another feller in the back and not give one damn about doing it. Bright was cut from the same cloth, only he was a lot faster than The Kid.

As they rode west against the hammering rain, Bitters conjured up pictures in his mind of old Elam Jordan swinging from a limb with a rope around his neck, or staked out on an anthill while the Apaches cut off his ears and nose. Then he started drawing the same mind pictures about Vent Torrey and the more he thought about the gunfighter, the more he realized if it hadn't been for him all this would never have happened. He wouldn't be riding through the damn rain, half a month's wages in his pocket, sided by a kid who thought he was Bill Bonney. Instead, he'd be up in that line shack sitting by the fire drinking coffee and drawing good money for doing nothing.

Turning, he looked at The Kid, then pulled in his horse and waiting until he did the same, leaned over and shouted against the howling wind, "I'm going after Leatherhand. I'm gonna kill the bastard."

The Kid stared at him. "You're crazy," he shouted back, turning his horse in an attempt to keep the driving rain out of his face.

"You can ride along or take off," Bitters said.

Without waiting for The Kid's answer, he turned his horse and rode on. The Kid followed, his head down, his hatbrim covering his eyes. As Bitters rode along, he flexed his wrist and decided it was about healed.

Far to the west Stalls stood in the barn of the Uvada Stage Station and stared down at Powers and Hall. Hall's face was covered with sweat. For two days now he had been in and out of delirium and Stalls knew if he didn't get him to a doctor, he'd probably die. Powers was in little better shape.

"Whitey, hitch up a team and fill a wagon with hay,"

he said, suddenly making a decision he knew he should have made a day ago.

Whitey turned from his position at a window and went out to the corral behind the barn for a team. Looking at Bright, Stalls said sourly, "Bobby, I want you to drive Hance and Roy to Cedar City. There should be a doc there."

Half an hour later Stalls stood at the rear door of the barn and watched Bright drive the team east. Although the wagon was plainly visible from the station, no shots were fired and Stalls wondered at that. He also wondered at the fact Torrey only wounded Powers and Hall. He knew that both men would now be dead if Torrey had willed it. He was too good to miss at that range.

Turning back, he went to the front door to take up his vigil.

Chapter Five

Carroll Rose shuffled the deck expertly and dealt the cards around, the soft sound of the pasteboards across the felt-covered table vaguely audible above the din of the drinkers in the Post Hole Saloon. Looking around, Rose automatically catalogued the patrons, looking for anyone who might pose a danger to him. He was seated in the gunfighter's chair with his back to the wall, having politely requested upon entering the game that the man sitting there turn it over to him. When the player belligerently refused, Rose smiled and walked to the bar, where he ordered a drink and stood balancing it in his right hand while he watched the game, a slight smile on his face.

Then one of the players leaned over and spoke to the man with his back to the wall, and that worthy hastily rose and came to the bar and, face white, said, "Mr. Rose, sorry about the misunderstanding. I'll be more than happy to change seats with you."

Rose nodded gravely and went to the table, sat down and, handing a sheaf of bills to the dealer, waited until his chips were counted out, then stacked them before him and settled down to play poker.

As the fifth card fell, Rose set the deck before him, lifted a chip from the pile, and placed it on top and picked up his hand. He held a pair of aces and three junk cards.

Wondering whether he should ask for one card and run a bluff or try to fill the hand, he decided to go for three when the door swung wide and the marshal of Cedar City came in and went to the bar. Glancing at the bartender, he ordered whiskey, then nodded at the man next to him and said, "Hello, Randolph, how are you?"

"Fine," Randolph said, then looking pointedly at the whiskey glass, observed, "Hell, Marshal, you don't usually drink this early in the morning."

"Just seen something kinda tough. . . . Feller came in from Uvada with a wagon. Was hauling two gents who were all shot to hell . . ."

"Who did it?"

"Feller name of Vent Torrey. The man driving the wagon, name of Bobby Bright, said he works for the Barbed-T ranch over east of the divide. He claims this Vent Torrey shot both fellers without giving them a chance."

Rose bet a hundred dollars and was called by three of the players. Flipping the hand over he displayed three aces, and when no one challenged the hand, raked in the pot, said quietly to the dealer, "Play around me for a bit," stood up and walked out the door.

Pausing on the sidewalk, he was in time to see Bobby Bright drive the wagon into the livery stable and, flipping the tiedowns from his pistol hammers, moved after him.

Inside, he found Bright and the liveryman unharnessing the team. Rose stepped in through the big double doors and to the left and paused until Bright, apparently feeling the gunman's eyes on him, suddenly looked up and then stepped away from the team. The liveryman, sensing a shooting, quickly led the team out through the back door and, jerking the harness off, turned them into a corral. Walking back into the barn, he stopped by his office and, leaning against the wall, watched the two men as they faced off.

Rose, his angelic face wreathed in a smile, said, "Mister, you are a damned liar. You told the marshal Vent Torrey shot two men from behind without giving them a chance. Leatherhand never shot a man in the back in his life. . . ."

Bright, still a liar even when faced with death, said sullenly, "He shot 'em from behind 'cause I saw it."

"Where was this at?" Rose asked.

"Why, at the Uvada Stage Station," Bright replied, his hand sneaking toward his gun butt. Rose ignored the move.

As he started to speak, a shadow fell across the entranceway to the barn and Rose, still watching Bright, glanced quickly to the right.

A man stood there quietly, his eyes riveted on Bright, who was staring back as if mesmerized.

Not looking at Rose, the man said softly, "My kill, Mr. Rose."

"You'll be Mick O'Reilly," Rose replied.

O'Reilly said nothing, merely staring at Bright. The cowboy, his face drained of all color, mumbled, "Wait, Mick, I don't know why you're here, but if the old man sent you, he's working on wrong information. I told him the truth. I swear to God I told him the truth."

"Then plead your case with God," O'Reilly said and drew as Bright made a desperate effort to get his gun into play. He was woefully slow.

As O'Reilly's slug tore into his guts and burst out through his spine, he screamed like a panther and, pistol pointed at the ground, triggered five shots. Then O'Reilly, taking his time, shot him again, this time through the forehead. As the big projectile drilled into Bright's brain, the cowboy was knocked spinning back into a stall where he left his death's blood splattered over the back wall and collapsed in the moldy straw, his face buried in horse manure.

"I never could stand a liar," O'Reilly said and replaced his spent rounds, turned and nodded at Rose and walked out.

Rose followed him through the door as the marshal came running up. Staring at the gunfighter, he said, "What happened in there?"

Rose, his smile still in place, shrugged and said, "You'll have to ask the liveryman," and walked around the marshal and through the small crowd, who had gathered at the sound of the shots. As he walked along the sidewalk, he saw O'Reilly turn into the telegraph office and thought, now he'll report to Elam Jordan, and entered the saloon. Going directly to the poker table, he sat down and smiling at the dealer, said quietly, "Deal me in."

As Bobby Bright kicked his last facedown in a dirty livery stable stall, his father, Longhorn Bull Bright, was just beginning the spring branding on his Circle-A ranch west of Shreveport, Louisiana, where the Bright family had lived and raised cattle, mules, and horses since before the War. Folks around that part of Louisiana left the Bright family strictly alone. They were known as feuders and barn burners and they stuck together against all common enemies.

Longhorn Bright hired fifteen riders, but the backbone of his outfit was his four sons, Cord, Tom, Abbot, and Canefield "Wild River" Bright, the oldest.

They were a hard bunch of men whose reputations with

the gun had been talked about in that part of the country for years. Canefield had been a sniper during the War and Tom and Abbot were cavalrymen. Cord rose to the rank of captain and received a number of decorations for bravery.

These were the kin of Bobby Bright and two days after O'Reilly's slugs put an end to his life, the marshal of Cedar City sent a telegram asking about the disposition of the body. He promptly received a return message requesting that it be placed on the train and sent along to Shreveport, where the Bright family would claim it and pay the freight.

Once Bobby, the youngest of the Brights, was safely interred in the family plot, Longhorn Bright called his clan together and announced, "Boys, we're going hunting up in Utah."

Two weeks later the train pulled into the depot at Cedar City and Longhorn and his four sons disembarked. They were followed off the train by nine Circle-A riders, all wearing two guns and toting rifles. The marshal witnessed this display of armament and wondered.

Singling out Longhorn, who was obviously the leader of the band, the marshal walked up, introduced himself and asked who they were.

"Mr. Marshal, my name's Longhorn Bright and these are my sons and my men," and the marshal thought, death has come to Cedar City.

Marshal Dan Stump was no coward, but he recognized trouble beyond his capabilities to handle when he saw it, and decided that he would not interfere unless this bunch started shooting up the citizens of the town.

Apparently guessing Stump's thoughts, Bright said, "You ain't got no worries about us. We ain't gonna hooraw your town. You tell me who pulled the trigger on Bobby and we'll handle him and be on our way."

"It won't be quite that easy, Mr. Bright," Stump said.

"Oh?"

"You see," Stump explained, "this Mick O'Reilly who killed your boy, he works for the Barbed-T over to South Pass City. Old Elam Jordan owns half the state over there and keeps about forty riders year around. He sets a great store by that Irishman."

Digging out a cigar and glancing at his four attentive sons, Bright asked, "Now why would Elam Jordan want Bobby dead?"

Stump didn't like this and it was obvious to Bright. "Look here, Marshal, I asked you a question. I want an answer," the old man snapped.

"They was only two fellers seen that shooting," Stump finally told him. "One was the liveryman and he up and left town on a high old lope. The other gent was Carroll Rose."

"Carroll Rose! What the hell has he got to do with this?" Bright asked, almost biting the end off his cigar.

"I don't rightly know," Stump said. "You see, your boy brought a couple of Barbed-T riders into town that day all shot to hell. When he went to put the wagon away at the livery, Rose went down there. Then O'Reilly showed up and the liveryman told me Rose was on the edge of going to the gun with your boy but that O'Reilly insisted he was his game."

"Who are these Barbed-T riders?" Bright asked.

"Roy Powers and Hance Hall," Stump answered. "They're over at the doc's mending. Both of them damned near died."

"Son-of-a-bitch," Bright snarled. "This here mess has got more quirks than a Mississippi River gambler. Who shot them two Barbed-T riders?"

"Feller they call Leatherhand," Stump replied, watching Bright's face.

"Leatherhand! Well, I'll be double-damned," Bright said in amazement. "Here we got Bobby shot dead by a Barbed-T gunny right after he brings in two Barbed-T riders who have been all shot to hell by Leatherhand and then Carroll Rose, he's in this too . . ."

Stump scratched his head. "I know it seems kinda queer, but the way I heard it Barbed-T has some kinda grudge against Leatherhand and he's riding with Denton Rose, young Carroll's daddy. They corraled the two at the Uvada Stage Station and Leatherhand plugged Powers and Hall. The Barbed-T segundo, Cap Stalls, sent your boy to town with the wounded men. Carroll Rose was here gambling at the Post Hole Saloon. He braces your boy and up and calls him a liar. Then in walks O'Reilly and he calls him a liar and they go to the gun."

"Where's Rose now?" Bright asked.

"Why, he's over at the Post Hole still playing poker," Stump said.

"What happened to O'Reilly?"

"Rode out half an hour after the shooting . . . I had no reason to hold him, what with two witnesses saying your boy went to his gun."

Canefield, a chew of tobacco bulging one cheek, stepped forward and said, "Hell, Paw, Bobby sure didn't have much chance with both O'Reilly and that Carroll Rose standing in line to shoot him."

Glancing at his oldest son, Bright observed, "Bobby, he never was much on brains and he did lie like hell. That's why I ran him off. But he was my son and I want to know what right O'Reilly's got going around shooting a Bright."

Turning, he called to one of the Circle-A riders, "Hank, you boys go on up town and get something to eat, then I want you to pick up enough grub over at the mercantile to carry us a few days. You, Arnie, you go find a couple of good pack mules, you hear?''

After the men had left, Bright told his sons, ''Come along,'' and, mounting his big blue roan gelding, led his boys down street and pulled up in front of the Post Hole Saloon. Dismounting, Bright led the way through the front door and, stopping just inside, looked the place over, spotted Carroll Rose playing poker at a table in the back of the room and trudged on down, his long-shanked Mexican spurs jingling musically as he stopped across from the smiling gambler and hands on hips, said, ''Mr. Rose, I'm Longhorn Bright. Bobby Bright was my son.''

Still smiling, Rose looked up and deep in his eyes something began to twist and turn as he said mildly, ''Then you had a liar for a son.''

As the words were spoken, men began drifting out the front and back doors and the dancehall girls scuttled up a set of stairs leading to the second floor, where they paused and, leaning on the hall rail, peered down at the big man with the lined face and the handlebar mustache.

''Pretty hard words, Mr. Rose,'' Bright observed.

''Call,'' Rose intoned and flipping up his cards, displayed aces and eights and a king kicker. Looking at them, his smile broadened. ''The death hand,'' he said softly and, raising his eyes to meet Bright's, asked, ''Yours or mine?''

''It needn't be either one of us,'' Bright said, keeping his hands well away from his guns.

Now the thing hiding in Rose's eyes was up and poised and Bright, looking into those insane orbs, suddenly knew that this man would take on him and all four of his sons and not give one damn whether he lived or died and for the first time in his long and dangerous life, Longhorn Bright was frightened. Rose might not give a damn if he lived or died, but Bright did.

Carefully now, he asked, "You, Mr. Rose, were a witness to my son's killing. Mind telling me what happened?"

Rose smiled and then looking around at the other players, said, "Gentlemen, I wish to apologize for this interruption of our game," and turning back to Bright, told him, "Your son came in town with two wounded men. He told the city marshal they had been shot from behind by Vent Torrey. My Paw is with Mr. Torrey and if you know of him, you also know he would never condone shooting anyone from behind. He is not a bushwacker. Neither is Mr. Torrey, whose reputation for fair play is widely known. Your son lied, but why is the question. I intended to ask him that, but he didn't live long enough."

"Did this fellow O'Reilly say why he killed my boy?" Bright asked.

Rose shook his head. "He did not. He merely rode out of town."

Suddenly, Bright decided Carroll Rose was lying, that there was a great deal more to all this than he was admitting. Glancing at his sons, he said harshly, "Mr. Rose, I am aware of your fearsome reputation, but my son is dead. I believe you are lying to me. I want answers . . ."

Carroll Rose did not answer. Instead he went into instant action, whipping up the Russian .44 and drilling Longhorn Bright squarely through the chest. Before the old man hit the floor and while the other players were still diving for cover, he shot Cord through the left eye and Tom through the stomach. Abbot Bright managed to clear his gun, but died with it in his hand as Rose, dropping behind the overturned table, shot him in the heart. The slug tore out his back and struck a spittoon, sending a hollow clatter through the room.

Canefield Bright had been standing to the right of his

father when the shooting began and had begun his draw, only to have it spoiled when Longhorn Bright, dying on his feet, spun and crashed into him, pitching him sideways. Now he swung up his pistol, but couldn't see Rose through the boiling powder smoke that filled the room.

Firing at where he thought the table was, he heard a man scream and did not know he had killed one of the players. Then the front door slammed back on its hinges and the room was full of Circle-A riders, guns in hand. Crouching, they waited until the smoke rose to the ceiling, then stood appalled. The area around the card table resembled a Chicago slaughterhouse. Bodies were sprawled everywhere, their life's blood smearing their clothes in streaks of crimson. A soft moaning came from the prostrate form of Tom Bright, who lay amid the carnage clutching his bullet-punctured stomach in agony.

Rose was nowhere to be seen.

Canefield, looking around wildly, suddenly pointed at the back door and shouted, "The back door. Rose went out that way. Get him."

As the Circle-A riders rushed out into the alley, Canefield knelt by his dying brother and tried to comfort him. Then Dan Stump was leaning over his shoulder.

"Better get the boy down to the doc's office," Stump counseled.

Canefield looked around at the marshal and shook his head bleakly. "No need now, he's dead," and he stood up, walked to the other members of his family and had his look, and then went to the bar and the bartender set him up a drink without being asked. Looking over the rim, he said softly, "Who'd have ever thought a man could be that damn fast?"

The next day Canefield Bright supervised the loading of his father and his brothers' bodies into a baggage car bound for Shreveport, while Stump looked on. As the train pulled out, the elder Bright walked down the platform to where his men stood or squatted in the dust, their horses saddled and waiting.

"We're going after two men, boys: Carroll Rose and Mick O'Reilly. Any of you fellers want out of this, I'll not hold it against you. Ride out now and I'll pay you off and shake hands goodby," Canefield said, and watched the men. No one said anything.

"Then git mounted," and walking to his father's big blue roan, he gathered up the reins and stepped aboard and led his men down the main street of Cedar City as Marshal Stump watched him go.

As soon as the line of riders cleared town, Stump hurried across to the telegraph office and closed the door behind him.

Vent was tired of the game Stalls was playing. Until now he hadn't wanted to kill any of the Barbed-T riders. He had no quarrel with them and did not hold it against them for carrying out orders. A man that wasn't loyal to his brand was no man at all, Vent knew, and so accepted the fact that Stalls and his men, even though trying to kill or capture him, were true to their outfit.

No shots had been fired for almost three hours and Vent wondered what Stalls was waiting for. Then Jeff Kidder rode into the stage station, dismounted, and entered the barn through the front door. Looking around at Denton Rose, Vent shook his head. "Feller sure as hell's taking a chance, now ain't he?"

"Probably figure we ain't much shuckins," Rose said with a smile.

Then Stalls stepped from the barn waving a white cloth

on a pitchfork handle. As he walked into the open, Whitey Beard and Kidder followed, their holsters empty.

Vent walked to the door, opened it, and stepped onto the porch. Rose and Bill Tatum came out and leaned against the side of the building. Both kept their rifles at the ready.

"Well, Mr. Stalls, you tired of this foolishness?" Vent asked.

Stalls grinned frostily. "Nope, me, I was enjoying the fandango, but Mr. Jordan sends his regards and asks me to apologize to you. It seems he discovered Bright, Bitters and Kid Calamity lied, a fact I could have enlightened him on before this all started if he had listened. He didn't and now we got two badly wounded men . . ."

Looking into his eyes, Vent said mildly, "I could have killed them just as easy."

Stalls nodded. "I know that."

Vent looked at Beard and asked, "This over for you, Whitey?"

"I follow orders," Beard said.

"What about you, Kidder? You agree?"

Kidder nodded.

"You boys had anything to eat since this started?" Vent asked.

Stalls looked at the ground, then said, "We dreamed about a big steak and chewed some grass stems."

Glancing at Tatum, Vent asked, "Mr. Tatum, think you can put us a meal together?"

"I can if I can find a pot or pan that ain't been holed," he said sourly and turned back inside.

Vent looked pointedly at the men's empty holsters and observed, "This here's a bad place to go around unarmed. Injuns might come ridin' down on us. You fellers best get your guns," and he went inside.

As they ate in silence, Tatum, carrying a plate loaded down with steak and potatoes, walked to the door and looked out, then announced, "Rider coming."

Vent looked up and asked, "Know him?"

Tatum shook his head. "Don't know him from Adam's off ox. Big feller packing two guns. Got on a fancy calfskin vest."

Stalls turned and rose and walked to the door, had his look, then came back and said, "Mick O'Reilly. Works for us."

Vent had heard of O'Reilly and so now he rose and went to the bar and asked Tatum for a bottle, keeping his eyes on the door. Seeing this Stalls said quietly, "No need for that. O'Reilly's not here looking for trouble," and then the Irishman walked in and seeing Stalls, said, "Got Elam's telegram, huh?"

"We got it," Stalls said.

Looking at Vent, O'Reilly inclined his head and noted, "You'll be Vent Torrey . . ."

"I'm Torrey," Vent agreed.

"Howdy, Denton," O'Reilly greeted the older man. "You're a far piece from Texas."

"Man does get around sometimes," Rose said.

"Met your boy at Cedar City. He was fixing to croak Bobby Bright. I saved him the trouble."

"Oh?" Stalls raised an eyebrow.

"He lied," O'Reilly said simply.

No more was said and the two factions remained at the stage station two more days, then a man got off the westbound stage, the first through in almost a week and, while drinking a whiskey, told Tatum, "Hell of a thing down at Cedar City. The Circle-A up from Shreveport jumped Carroll Rose in the Post Hole Saloon. When the smoke cleared away, the boy had done for old Longhorn

Bull Bright and three of his sons and got clean away without a scratch. I tell ya mister, that barroom was so fulla flying lead the only safe place was under the floor. Hell, one of them Brights even plugged a bystander and killed him dead as a nit.''

"What started it anyway?" one of the passengers asked.

Will Splevins, the stage driver, spoke up and said, "They come to town looking for the man that killed Bobby Bright. Said they was gone to put him under. Them there Brights come from feudin' stock. Never forget . . .''

"Well, they ain't forgot now either,'' the westbound passenger said. "The only one of the Brights to survive, Canefield, I believe they call him, took off with nine of the Circle-A punchers announcing high and wide that two men was going to the grave now. He named Mick O'Reilly and Carroll Rose.''

"I reckon it's all up for me,'' O'Reilly said in an aside to Stalls, who grinned and decided they had best pull out and find a telegraph office.

After the stage left, Vent stood up and, looking at Denton, said, "Mr. Rose, this ain't finding your boy.''

Rose nodded then, shaking his head, observed, "I ain't too sure I wanta find him,'' and followed Vent out the door.

They were half a mile along the road to Nevada when Stalls and his men overtook them. "Decided Pioche's the nearest telegraph office. Mind if we join you?''

Vent grinned. "Rather have you riding with me than shooting at me.''

Elam Jordan rode into Cedar City backed by twenty Barbed-T riders. As the white-haired old man pulled his horse up in front of the marshal's office and his men formed a semi-circle behind him, Stump stepped onto the sidewalk, had his look at the hard-looking bunch of punchers and said mildly, "If you've come to conquer Cedar City, Mr. Jordan, I doubt you'll get much resistance."

Jordan smiled his frosty smile and observed, "Not to slight your town any, neighbor, but I'm damned if I can figure out why a man would want to conquer this place."

"We do have some fairly rich mines around here, but the Army kinda looks after them," Stump said.

Stepping down, Jordan followed the marshal into his office and when the door was closed, went and turned a chair around and sat astradle it as Stump stepped behind his battered desk and sat down. Digging around in a drawer, he finally unearthed a dust-covered whiskey bottle and holding it up to the light from the window, peered through it, then blew away the dust and handed it to Jordan.

"Sorry, but I don't have a clean glass in the place," and watched Jordan tip the bottle and drain away a third of it and hand it back.

"That's some panther piss," the old man observed.

Stump drank, lowered the bottle and said, "You got my telegram, I see."

"I got it. Fill me in."

Half an hour later Jordan walked out on the sidewalk and, nodding at one of the men, ordered, "Charlie, you take the boys down to the saloon and see that they get one drink," and turned and walked south until he reached the doctor's office and entered.

Milo Sims had been the only doctor for a hundred miles around since the first day he appeared at Cedar City. He had patched up gunshot victims, knife slashes, had delivered over a hundred babies, had nursed folks through a typhoid outbreak, and watched a third of the babies he delivered die. Now he looked up at Jordan and observed, "You look too damn healthy to be coming to a doctor."

"I'm Elam Jordan," the rancher said. "You got a couple of my boys here. I want to see them and I want to pay their bill."

Doc turned and led Jordan down the hall and into a room where Powers and Hall occupied neighboring beds. Looking them over, Jordan observed, "Looks to me like you fellers may just make it."

Hall grinned a weak grin and looking at Powers, said, "If this here ranahan don't quit his damn cheating at cards, you're gonna lose a man anyway."

Jordan turned to Powers and looking him over, said, "If you've got enough energy to cheat at cards, I reckon you'll be ready to get back to work in a few days."

"Work! What the hell's that?" Powers asked, looking flabbergasted.

Hall turned to him and explained, "You know, that's where Mr. Jordan pays you too much money for doing too little."

Glancing at the doctor, Jordan nodded his head and led the way down the hall and stopped long enough to pay Sims, thank him for taking care of Powers and Hall, and then headed back up street, where he found half the town turned out staring at his men.

Mounting up, he looked them over, said, "Let's ride," and turned his horse west.

They rode into the Uvada Stage Station the next day and found Bill Tatum sitting on the front veranda cleaning his rifle. As Jordan pulled up in front of the place, Tatum looked up and said, "You'll be Elam Jordan. There's water in the trough and grain in the barn. Help yourself. I'll put on the bean pot," and rose and went inside.

When the men finished taking care of their horses and

tramped into the stage station, they found twenty places set at the long wooden table and a huge pot of beans spiced with large chunks of beef sitting in the middle of the table. Platters of steaks hot off the stove were scattered the length of the board and piles of biscuits in pans sided by bowls of gravy awaited the men.

Leaning against the bar, Tatum asked, "Any of you boys want whiskey?"

Jordan looked up and shook his head. "We'll have a pot of coffee and a drink after we eat."

Tatum nodded, then said, "I'm Bill Tatum. I manage this shebang," and, not waiting for introductions, went and fetched the coffee, filling each man's cup himself.

When the Barbed-T crew finished, the table resembled a disaster area. Not one bean or steak remained and the biscuits had vanished as if they had never been. There was no gravy left and even the hot peppers Tatum had supplied were gone.

Jordan looked up at Tatum and said, "Now we'll have that drink, Mr. Tatum," and the station manager brought a bottle and a tray of clean glasses. Again he served the men.

Each rider picked up his glass and waited for Jordan. The rancher lifted his, drained it and his men followed suit.

Rising, Jordan walked to the bar and asked, "Mr. Tatum, how much do I owe you?"

Tatum named a price and Jordan nodded, said, "That's fair," and counted the money out in gold coin. Looking into Tatum's eyes then, he asked softly, "Some of my boys spent a few days here. Seems they was doing some shooting and you, Mr. Tatum, and Vent Torrey and Denton Rose was also doing some shooting. I called my boys off. I need to know two things; do I owe you anything for damages and which way did Cap Stalls go?"

Tatum thought a moment, then said, "You owe me nothing, Mr. Jordan. Your men rode west. So did Leatherhand and Denton Rose. Denton was looking for his son."

"I thank you, sir," Jordan said, "and will take this opportunity to apologize for the mistake. It was my fault and I take the blame."

"You have no problem with me, sir," Tatum said, then added as Jordan turned to leave, "but you will someday have to face Vent Torrey. He is not a man to forget."

"I expect that," was all Jordan said.

Chapter Six

The silver-mining town of Pioche was a misshapen scatter
of board, rock, and tin miner's shacks lining a narrow,
twisty canyon on the eastern slopes of the Highland
Mountains. It had once hosted eight thousand roistering
miners, teamsters, whores, pimps, gamblers, flash gunmen
and the real article, mining engineers from the east, and
top-hat–wearing dignitaries from as far away as San Fran-
cisco and New York. Each of this collection of humans
played a role in wrestling over a hundred million dollars from
the rocky ground that had concealed some of the richest silver
mines in the world and in one case, the richest such mine in
the nation. Each mine had its stamp mills grinding away
twenty-four hours a day, in one instance sixty of them in a
valley and owned by one company. There was a District Court,
a courthouse that cost the Lincoln County taxpayers over a
million dollars before the bonds were finally laid away,
and a sheriff who banked $40,000 a year in bribe money.
The town claimed a man a week during its growing pains.
Now it sat in silent witness to what happens when the vein
plays out. There were still things happening in the town,

but not at the rate they had occurred during Pioche's heyday.

It was into this still-wild town Vent Torrey and Denton Rose rode one Sunday morning. They put their horses up at the Dexter Stables on Main Street and went in search of a hotel, finding several.

Turning into the first one they came to, Vent tramped up to the desk, spun the register and signed his name, then stepped back while the clerk waited boredly. Denton Rose signed and turned the register back and the clerk glanced at the names, did a classic double take and, looking up at Vent, said hesitantly, "Welcome to the Creole House, gentlemen . . . be staying long?"

"Don't know," Vent said and waited for his key.

The clerk let his eyes fall to Vent's right hand, stared at the odd leather glove he wore there for a long moment, then, when Vent said, "The keys," jumped and turned and pulled two keys from their boxes and handed them over.

"Send up some hot water," Vent said and, carrying his saddle bags and rifle, led the way upstairs.

While Vent and Rose were catching up on lost sleep, a lone rider dressed in gambler's attire and wearing two guns, one across his belt buckle and the other in the conventional hip holster, rode slowly down the twisty turns of Main Street, looking at the wild profusion of shacks, business establishments, and dozens of saloons as he made his way to the first hotel he saw. Rounding into the hitch rack, he dismounted and stepped up on the wooden sidewalk, looked both ways, then entered the lobby, stopped again to check its occupants and, seeing nothing more dangerous than a drummer sitting in a corner reading a three-months-old *Sacramento Bee* newspaper, walked to the desk, turned the register and signed his name with a flourish.

"My horse is tied outside," he said. "He's the one wearing the black saddle and bridle. Have him taken care of for me, will you?"

The clerk spun the register, glanced down at the name and back at his smiling guest and said, "Yes sir, Mr. Rose. Would you like bath water?"

Carroll Rose, still smiling, nodded gravely, accepted the key and went upstairs and along a hall, found his room and entered.

Twenty minutes later as he slid deep into the washtub full of hot water, he leaned back, checked to make sure he was able to reach his guns swiftly, and lit the cigar he had thoughtfully placed on the same chair his weapons hung from.

While Carroll Rose reclined thus, two men hauled in their weary horses atop a hill overlooking Pioche and sat slouched in their saddles gazing dispiritedly down at the mean collection of shacks.

"Ain't much is it?" Tag Bitters observed.

"Beats the hell outa sleeping out in the damn rain," Kid Calamity countered.

They put their horses to the slope and entered the town from the north. Bitters rode directly to a house set a hundred feet off Main Street back up a side canyon and dismounted. Going to the door, he knocked and waited. A long minute passed, then a woman came out, looked at Bitters, said, "Well, if it ain't the prodigal son. Where the hell did you come from?"

"From over east of the divide," Bitters said. "Been working on a spread over there."

The woman sighed and said, "Put your horses out back and come on in. . . . Who's the wet-ear you got with ya?"

The Kid's face grew red as he stared meanly at her, then she patted his cheek and said, "Never mind, darlin', mama loves them young and tender," and nodded at Bitters and went back inside.

Bitters grinned. "My sister," he said.

Monday morning Cap Stalls led his men into Pioche. They had spent the night camped outside town. Going directly to the telegraph office Stalls leaned on the counter and said, "Name's Stalls. Got anything for me?"

The clerk, a slightly built man who talked with a lisp, fumbled in a pile of forms, finally unearthed one and handed it to the Barbed-T segundo. Stalls pushed his hat on the back of his head and read it, then turned and went out and stepped into the saddle. Wordlessly, he led his men south again and half a mile from town rode up a side canyon and climbed down.

"We wait," he said.

Canefield Bright sat by a campfire outside Bennett's Wells just south of Pioche and waited for the man he had sent into the mining town to return and report. They had passed through Panaca, a once-lively mining town that was now about played out. Canefield asked questions and, when the men he questioned looked at his hard-bitten crew, they answered respectfully and honestly. Yes, they had seen three men ride through town and one of them had been Whitey Beard. They had also recognized the man called Vent Torrey and one man, braver than the rest, said he had spotted Carroll Rose riding toward Pioche right after noon.

Now Bright waited for his man and made careful plans.

As he waited patiently, Elam Jordan led his small army into Clover Valley near Pioche and stopped at a ranch house where he was quickly invited in by its owner, a man who had once worked for him before starting his own spread. Jordan's men camped out in the barn and the yard and, looking at them scattered around the place armed with enough guns to take Mexico, Jordan thought, nobody can stand against us. He had sent a man to gather up Stalls and his men and bring them back.

The stage was set and the marshal of Pioche, a quiet man who said little but was long on action, gazed out his window and thought about all the information that had trickled to him and wondered what the hell was going on.

Looking around at his deputy, he said, "Shelton, this here mess is gettin' messier. Here we got Leatherhand and some gent name of Rose at the Creole House; we got Carroll Rose at the Tunnel Hotel and two strangers at Maude Bitters' place. South of here a whole damn army is camped at Bennett Springs and north of us, old Elam Jordan from over to South Pass City is holed up at Ira Spence's ranch in Clover Valley. Then we got those fellers down in the canyon, one of 'em being none other than Whitey Beard."

Shelton Thomas was glad he wasn't the marshal. That's what they paid Port Paley for. So he merely shook his head and observed, "Hell, maybe they're just passing through."

Paley stared at him for a long minute, then observed, "I reckon I keep forgetting the reason I hired you, Shelton. It wasn't because of your superior deductive powers, that's for sure."

Looking puzzled, Thomas asked, "Why did you hire me?"

"Christ," Paley groaned. "Because, dammit, you're my brother-in-law."

"So, what do we do now?"

"We wait," Paley said and poured a cup of coffee from

the blackened pot on the swollen-gutted stove crouching in its sandbox in the middle of the room.

Vent sat in the dining room of the Creole House and ate steak and eggs and wondered how Denton Rose was making out. The ex-rancher had left early that morning to look the town over and see if he could get a line on his son.

Halfway through his breakfast Vent, with that instinct nurtured by his profession, felt eyes on him, looked up and saw an average-appearing man with a round face and quiet eyes making his way through the morning diners. As he passed tables, he was greeted by friendly jibes or cheery hellos, then he reached Vent's table and stopped and said quietly, "Mr. Torrey, you mind if I join you?"

"As long as you pay for your own breakfast," Vent said and grinned faintly.

Sliding into a chair the man glanced toward an approaching waitress. "I'm the town marshal here. Name's Port Paley," and then a pretty blonde girl wearing an apron was at their table and Paley smiled at her and asked, "When you gonna give an old man a break and go to the opry house with me?"

She smiled, removed his hat and kissed him on a bald spot on top of his head as the diners sitting around them chuckled, and said, "Why, Mr. Marshal, I'd take it right handsome if you'd escort me to the next opry. . . ." then she looked sad and added, "but you know how Paw is. Keeps that there old shotgun of his oiled and ready all the time. Just can't wait to nail me a husband."

"I reckon it'd be worth it to lose my freedom," Paley answered, walling his eyes.

Smiling, the waitress observed, "Lovesick folks need their strength. What you gonna have this morning," and she glanced at Vent, got caught in his bottomless eyes and stared as if mesmerized.

Looking at her, Paley said gently, "If you can tear your eyes away from this poor wandering traveler for one minute, I'll order," and her face grew red as she jerked her eyes away from Vent, who merely continued to look at her.

After the girl had gone away with Paley's order, the marshal suddenly grew serious. "Mr. Torrey, I know your rep, as I reckon almost every lawman in the west does. I also know you are a fair man, that you lawed some yourself and that you never hire your gun.

"Now, some funny things are building up in this town. It's my town and my responsibility. I'm hired to keep the citizens safe. I'm also hired to keep track of what's happening in my jurisdiction. Now I ain't a feller to talk about another man's duty, but our sheriff, well, he's a politician first and a lawman last. You understand?"

Vent nodded. "Seen a few . . ."

"I know it's none of my damn business why you're here, but you're part of a puzzle that I've lost a piece to," Paley observed.

The waitress brought the marshal's food then and, after teasing her again, he fell to and, between mouthfuls, glanced at Vent and asked, "Did you know that Elam Jordan and about twenty of his men are north of town at a ranch in Clover Valley?"

Vent looked at him sharply, then shook his head and waited.

"Down at Bennett Springs a feller name of Canefield Bright from Louisiana is camped with ten men and Carroll Rose is staying at the Tunnel Hotel."

"The hell you say?" Vent exclaimed, wondering if Denton Rose had finally found his son.

"Yep, and that ain't all," Paley went on. "Two fellers

hit town two days ago. Now normally I don't pay a lot of attention to drifters, but these two stopped over at Maude Bitters' house and have been there ever since. Maude makes her living by the light of the moon and these old boys don't seem to be staying there for that reason."

"Tag Bitters and a wet ear calling himself Kid Calamity," Vent said. "Tag's probably the woman's brother or some other relative."

"They got anything to do with you or any of these other fellers?" the marshal asked, watching Vent's face and finding nothing but a blank wall of flesh there.

"I had me a little run in with them at South Pass City," Vent explained. "That's what this here mess is all about," and briefly he sketched the past few weeks' happenings. When he finished, Paley shook his head and said, "I wonder if they could use a good marshal at Santa Fe or maybe Tombstone. It'd be a damn sight safer than this town's gonna be."

Vent drained his coffee cup and refilled it from the pot sitting at the edge of the table, then looking at Paley, observed, "The way I figure this is that those two at the whore's house are after me. Canefield Bright wants Carroll Rose and Mick O'Reilly. Elam Jordan is here to see that Bright doesn't get O'Reilly. Carroll Rose already wiped out most of the Bright family. He can take care of himself."

Clearing his throat Paley said quietly, "He's insane, you know."

"I figured that," Vent agreed, then looking Paley in the eye, added, "Ain't most of us that go to the gun?"

Paley, who had put down his share of men, said softly, "I reckon you're right, Mr. Torrey. A man'd have to be crazy to stick at this job."

"He'd have to be crazier to do it without pay," Vent observed drily.

"For money or for a friend, what's the difference?"

Then Shelton Thomas came in and walked to their table and Paley introduced him and Thomas sat down uninvited and looking at Vent, noted, "So you're the famous Leatherhand. Hell, mister, you look like just about any old cowpoke goin' down the road."

Paley stared at him and Vent grinned. Shaking his head, Paley said, "This here feller, he stays alive 'cause nobody takes him serious. The only reason I keep him on is because he's kin and he follows orders without bothering me with a lot of questions."

"Best kind of deputy to have," Vent said solemnly.

Glancing up then, he narrowed his eyes and observed, "Looks like we're about to have some company," and the marshal turned and had his look and turned back and leveled a cold eye on Thomas and ordered, "Don't you say one damn word to either one of these fellers. I can't afford to plant you right now and the town ain't got any money for burying deputies either."

Denton and Carroll Rose were approaching their table, the younger Rose looking for all the world as if he just stepped from a choir box and strapped on his daddy's guns to play cowboy. A soft smile was on his face and his eyes were filled with innocence. Vent couldn't help but note the sharp contrast between father and son. Denton Rose wore a patched pair of Levis covered with batwing chaps, a worn gunbelt, and a rough chambray shirt topped off with a battered Stetson hat jammed down on his grizzled graying hair. His son wore dark pants, a long-tailed gambler's coat, white linen, and a string tie. His gunbelt and his guns showed exceptional care and his boots had been recently blacked, where his father's were scuffed and scarred and the pair of OK spurs he wore tarnished by years of use. Carroll sported a fine pair of silver-mounted California spurs and Vent noted his hat was a triple-X beaver of the finest quality. He had to admit that Carroll Rose, what with his fine clothes, long gold hair, and beguiling eyes and smile, was a handsome young man. It was only when you looked into those eyes that the tiger lurking there showed itself, if ever so briefly.

Denton stopped at the table and nodding at the marshal, said, "This here's my boy, Carroll."

Vent looked up and nodded and turned to Denton and asked, "Had your breakfast?"

"Nope, and I'm ready. Mind if Carroll joins us?"

"Glad to have him," Vent said and meant it.

Paley looked at the two gunmen and suddenly felt terribly inadequate. There was something about these two men that made them stand out in a crowd, that commanded instant attention. It wasn't just the number of men they had laid away either. They had presence, something Paley figured a man acquired with time and experience . . . and managing to stay alive through a hundred gunfights.

Vent had chosen his table because it was situated against a far wall and now Carroll Rose took the chair nearest him, which also placed his back away from the diners and gave him a clear view of the entranceway and the street through the large front windows. Denton, not overly concerned about somebody shooting him in the back, sat facing Vent. Paley watched the positioning and smiled inwardly. A hell of a way for a man to have to live, always worrying about somebody sneaking up on him from behind. He recalled Morgan Courtney, a dandified outlaw who sold his gun to one of the local mining interests. He had rolled into Pioche some years back carrying a carpet bag and a Henry rifle, and wearing a pistol. When George McKinney killed him, he was wearing the same outfit he hit town with and it served as his burying clothes.

One of his partners, Mike Casey, plugged Tom Gorson and shortly thereafter Jim Levy, a Deadwood, South Dakota gunsel, shot and killed Casey. And so it went. One man killed another and then was killed in turn. With these thoughts, Paley was suddenly glad he wasn't the fastest man around.

Nodding at Paley, Vent introduced him to Carroll and the youthful gunman solemnly shook hands. No one bothered to introduce Thomas, who sat stolidly watching the proceedings. When the waitress came back to the table, she stared openly at Carroll, her eyes wide, as he stared back. Twice she dropped her pencil while taking their order and each time the younger Rose gallantly retrieved it for her. When she went away, her face was red and flustered and Carroll's smile was still in place.

While they waited for their food, Vent quietly filled the father and son in and Denton glanced at the marshal. "What do you make of all this?"

"Figure they's gonna be some shooting," Paley replied.

"Looks kinda that way," smiled Carroll.

Vent looked at Paley and remarked, "Marshal, it ain't my style to sit by while somebody hunts me. I figure Bitters and The Kid are here doing just that. I guess maybe I'll just look them up and have me a little talk, sorta try and convince them that this ain't the healthiest climate for fellers from South Pass City."

Then the waitress returned with their food and set plates before Carroll and Denton. As she started to turn somebody near the alcove leading to the hotel clerk's desk shouted. The shout was suddenly choked off as if the man's throat had been cut and Vent swept an arm around the girl's waist and pulled her down on the back side of the table as Bitters and The Kid burst into the dining room.

"You're dead, Leatherhand!" Bitters screamed and swung

a double-barreled, sawed-off shotgun up to his hip, its gaping bores a deathly threat to everyone in the room. The Kid held a .45 in each fist and as he stepped through the door, he raised the guns and leveled them at Vent's table.

Three things happened almost simultaneously. The girl hit the floor with a grunt, Vent drew like chain lightning and shot Bitters through the throat, and Carroll Rose whipped his belly gun across his body in a move so swift men later said they did not see him do it and shot The Kid through the left breast pocket, kicking dust from his shirtfront and knocking him sprawling, his pistols useless steel in hands that no longer felt. Bitters flipped backwards when hit by Vent's heavy .44 slug, landing on the back of his head and his shoulders, then collapsed over onto his side, drew his legs up and kicked them out in a futile protest against dying, and as blood burst from his gaping mouth to pour across the tile of the lobby, groaned and died.

Helping the girl to her feet, Vent said, "Sorry young lady, but I sure didn't want you to get hurt."

Rubbing her backside, she said, "That floor's hard . . . but I thank you, sir, for saving my life."

Turning then, she stared at the two dead men and the diners still huddled behind tables and flattened out on the floor and said, "Oh!" and hurried into the kitchen, still rubbing where she had bumped herself.

Punching out their empties, Vent and Carroll Rose reloaded. Both Thomas and Paley had gone for their guns when Bitters and The Kid first appeared, but were woefully slow, as was Denton Rose. He stood staring down at the unfired pistol in his hand and shaking his head, asked wonderingly, "Now why the hell did I even go for this damn thing?"

"You got the right instincts, Paw," smiled Carroll.

*   *   *

Elam Jordan was sitting on the veranda of Ira Spence's ranch house, his boots up on the rail, a cup of coffee in hand, when Stalls rode into the yard and dismounted, turning his horse over to one of the Barbed-T punchers. Watching him come across the yard, Jordan wished this damn thing had never gotten started. Behind Stalls, Whitey Beard and Mick O'Reilly, quietly talking together, came along, ignoring the jibes of their fellow punchers.

Stalls climbed the five steps to the veranda and Jordan nodded at a chair and invited, "Sit, Cap. Any news from town?"

"You can scratch Bitters and The Kid," he said.

Jordan looked keenly at O'Reilly. "You do them?"

"Leatherhand and Carroll Rose saved me the trouble," smiled O'Reilly and lit a thin Mexican cheroot and went and sat on the porch rail.

"So, what happened?" Jordan directed his question to Stalls.

"Those two idiots bust into the Creole House dining room, guns up, and ran right smack into Torrey and Rose sitting at a table. The feller that told me about it said it was a toss up as to which one of those boys got unlimbered first," Stalls related.

"The Kid or Bitters get off a shot?" Jordan asked.

"Nope. All those two did was fall down and die," Stalls said cryptically.

Then one of the Barbed-T riders called from the yard, "Rider coming in."

Jordan stood up and walked to the rail as Ira Spence came from the barn, a bridle dangling from one hand. As the horseman rounded into the yard, the sun struck instant fire from the sheriff's badge he wore and Jordan, who knew his share of lawmen, both good and bad, instantly pegged the man on the horse as all gurgle and no guts.

Pulling his horse up sharply, the lawman said, "I'm Dance Evers, sheriff of Lincoln County."

Jordan took his time looking the lawman over and what he saw brought a flicker of amusement to his cold eyes. Evers was fifty pounds overweight, had too much hair, a jowly face, thick, awkward-appearing hands, and wore clothes that must have set him back three hundred dollars. His gunbelt was studded with silver, as were the butt plates of the twin Frontier Colt .45s he wore. Large silver conchos studded the gunbelt and his leather hatband. His saddle was also silver-mounted and it sat on a beautiful Palomino gelding. The headstall and bit carried enough silver to finance a bank, and the long-shanked spurs snugged to the heels of a pair of Mexican bench-made boots with huge butterflies stitched in them had enough silver enlaid in them that Jordan guessed when the sheriff walked, they probably dragged out his tracks.

"I'm Elam Jordan from east of the divide over Wyoming way," he said, staring at the apparition in splendor sitting before him.

"My informants tell me you and your men are here to go to war with Canefield Bright and his crew," Evers said, and he made it an accusation.

Jordan sat down on the porch rail and, looking at the sheriff, let his eyes wander contemptuously over his finery and said distinctly, "I ain't saying one way or another, Mr. Evers, but if I was, I sure as hell wouldn't be dealing with no damn peacock."

Ignoring the insult, Evers leveled a finger at Jordan and snapped, "Now, you listen to me, Mr. Jordan. You got a man out here by the name of Mick O'Reilly. Canefield Bright has sworn out a warrant against him for murder. I'm taking him in."

Jordan grinned, and jerking a thumb in O'Reilly's direction, said calmly, "There he stands. Hop to it."

Evers whirled his horse around to face O'Reilly and said, "You, shuck them guns and get mounted. You're going to jail."

"The hell you say?" O'Reilly marveled, staring at the duded-up lawman.

"That's right, mister pistoleer, and don't start anything. You do and I'll have fifty men out here and clean up this bunch."

O'Reilly strolled along the porch, stopped at the top of the steps and asked curiously, "How the hell you gonna do that when you're dead?"

Evers stared at him. "Now wait just a dad-blamed minute here," he shouted. "I'm the sheriff of this county. You shoot me and you'll never see Wyoming again."

O'Reilly dropped his hand to his gun and said, "I reckon I'll just chance that, mister blowhard," and he drew swiftly, leveled the gun at the sheriff, and eared the hammer back. The sound of the double-click was heard clearly by the men leaning against the corral clear across the yard.

Holding up both hands, the sheriff said, "Hey now, I ain't out here to get into no gunfight with a shootist. I got me a legal warrant."

O'Reilly only smiled, then Spence came up and looking at the sheriff, observed, "Dance, you are a damn fool. Who put you up to this trick?"

Looking down at Spence, Evers said plaintively, "I got me a warrant, Ira."

"Warrant ain't worth doodly squat here in Nevada," Spence said reasonably. "O'Reilly plugged the Bright kid at Cedar City. That's Utah's jurisdiction. This feller Canefield Bright just want's you to pull his irons outa the fire. I suppose he swore out a warrant for Carroll Rose, too?''

''Well, yes, he did. Hell, Rose, he's a damned killer. Bumped off Bright's whole family,'' Evers said.

Spence stared up at him then shook his head. ''Dance, how the hell do you figure to serve the warrant on Rose?''

''Why, just walk up and serve it. I got me the power of the court ridin' my cantleboard.''

Shaking his head, Spence walked up the steps, making certain he did not get between O'Reilly and the sheriff, and told Jordan, ''You see what happens when the politicians buy a sheriff. You get his kinda thing.''

Evers' face grew red as he said loudly, ''Now see here, Ira, I heard that. No man buys Dance Evers. No man.''

''Can it, Dance,'' Spence advised. ''You was bought long before the first vote was cast. Now, if this feller Canefield Bright paid you to serve these warrants, then he paid for your death warrant because if Mick here don't fill you fulla lead, Carroll Rose damn sure will. That boy don't wait around to palaver. He just shoots. If he don't get you, why Vent Torrey will.''

''Who the hell is Vent Torrey?'' Evers demanded.

''See what I mean?'' Spence asked Jordan. ''Feller don't know nothin' and ain't got a lick of sense. Probably be dead in a day or so . . . .''

''He will be if he jumps Carroll Rose,'' O'Reilly commented.

Jordan glanced at O'Reilly, who still stood with his gun leveled on the sheriff's chest and then looked at the sheriff and asked, ''You still wanta haul Mick here off to jail?''

''I can't haul him anywhere long as he's standing there pointing that damned hogleg at me,'' Evers objected plaintively.

''Well, sheriff, I don't own this spread, but if I did, I'd

tell you to haul your damn freight outa here and go back and tell that Louisiana Frenchy he best head home 'cause all he's gonna find here is a hole in the ground,'' Jordan counseled.

Spence nodded. ''That's my sentiments exactly, Dance. You go on back to town and tell Mr. Canefield Bright that since he saddled this bronc, it's up to the Circle-A to ride him.''

''It's your funeral,'' Evers grumbled and turning his horse, rode from the yard, his back straight as a ramrod. Watching him go, Jordan observed, ''Now don't he look fancy?''

''Only problem with fancy is that it ain't tough,'' O'Reilly said and shoved his gun into leather and, looking at Spence, asked, ''Mr. Spence, suppose your cook could throw together something for me and the boys? Rations been kinda slim lately.''

''Hell yes, Mick. You boys go on over to the cook shack and tell Cookie I sent you,'' Spence told him then glanced up at the sun, cleared his throat, and looking at Jordan, asked, ''I suppose it's too early for a drink?''

Laughing deep in his throat, Jordan took Spence's arm and the two went inside. As they entered the big front room, Spence said, ''Oh, by the way. Wouldn't do to misjudge Evers.''

Vent, Carroll Rose, and Port Paley sat in the marshal's office and talked. Glancing out the window, Vent suddenly stood up, walked to the door and gazed out as Sheriff Dance Evers hauled his horse to a stop at the hitchrack and dismounted, waving at half a dozen men just riding away from one of the saloons. ''How you, Bob? Jack? Danny, you staying sober? Clemmy, you owe the judge a ten spot. Better come in next week and pay it,'' and not waiting for an answer, moved up the steps and when he saw Vent in the doorway, stopped short and looked him over, then asked, "Who the hell are you?"

Vent didn't have to think long before he decided he probably wasn't going to like Sheriff Dance Evers. Looking at the dandified lawman, he said distinctly, "None of your damn business," and turned and went back inside and sat down as the sheriff followed him in and closed the door. Staring at Vent, he snapped, "Mister, I'm the sheriff of this here county and I asked you a question. I want a civilized answer."

Vent stood up and walked over and stopped two feet from the lawman. Staring him in the eye, the Missourian slowly lifted both his guns from their holsters and, walking back to his seat, sat down and spun each of them on his finger, finding their balance bad. "Too much silver on these things, Mr. Sheriff. Makes for bad balance. You ever shoot one of these?"

Evers stepped forward and held out his hand and said sharply, "Hey, them's my guns. Hand 'em over, you damn peckerwood."

Shaking his head, Vent looked at Paley and asked, "Is everybody in this town stupid, or am I gettin' smarter?"

Paley leaned his chin on his elbow and, staring at Evers, said, "Funny thing about this here town. It just sorta attracts fellers like old Dance, here. Don't know where the hell they come from," and he winked at the sheriff.

Evers drew himself up to his full height and snapped, "By God, I know where I come from. I'm from Illinois."

Rose, who had walked to the door, now turned his head and said softly, "Bunch of fellers ridin' up the street . . ."

"Can I have my guns back?" Evers asked, looking over his shoulder.

Vent spun them by their trigger guards and handed them

over, then went to the door and had his look and said, "Tough-looking bunch . . ."

When he stepped away from the door, Evers strutted through, saying, "That there's them boys from Louisiana. I'll handle this," and walked out on the sidewalk, where he paused at the hitch rack and hands on hips, waited, his hat pushed to the back of his head.

Vent glanced at Paley. "That feller any good with them pistolos or just plain addled?"

"A little of both," Paley said. "In the first place, this ain't his jurisdiction. In the second place, they're gonna just naturally weight him down with lead. Too many of them for one man."

Having said that, Paley rose and went to the gun cabinet, where he selected a double-barreled shotgun and a box of shells. Breaking the deadly Greener, he pushed two double-ought buck rounds into its gaping barrels and walked to the door, standing just to the left of it as he watched the oncoming riders.

Vent took up a station by the window and Rose, removing his coat and carefully draping it over a peg on the wall, took the middle of the room where he could look directly into the street, then glancing around, saw a back door and, nodding at Vent, walked through it. Vent guessed he would cut down an alley and come up behind the Circle-A riders.

The sheriff stood his ground as Canefield Bright pulled rein in front of the office and sat glaring at him. "You lock O'Reilly and Rose up?" he asked.

"Found out I don't have jurisdiction over them," Evers said.

"So, they're still on the loose?"

"Yep, and Mr. Bright, you and your boys had best just

drift on outa here,'' Evers warned and Vent marveled at the man's gall.

Deciding he couldn't just stand by and watch the law-man cut down, Vent stepped onto the sidewalk and moved to the right, taking up a position five feet from Evers. As he did so, Paley walked out and, shotgun hanging from his fist, positioned himself on the left of the sheriff and waited.

Bright looked at Paley and observed, ''You must be Port Paley, the marshal here.''

''I am,'' Paley said.

Jerking a thumb toward where Vent stood leaning against a porch support, he asked, ''Who's that waddy? One of your deputies?''

Vent, his face cold and implacable, said softly, ''Mr. Bright, your brother was a damned fool looking for a place to get killed. I damned near did him myself once. Are you as much a damn fool as he was?''

Ignoring Paley and the sheriff, Bright centered his atten-tion on Vent, not sure what to make of this brash-talking man. ''Who're you?''

''You're the second fool who's asked me that in the past five minutes, mister. Who I am is none of your damn business and if you weren't a rank greenhorn, you'd know a man doesn't ask another who he is or where he comes from in this country. Because you are not from here, I'm willing to overlook the breech of politeness.''

''Oh, you are, are you,'' Bright snapped. ''Well now, that's right damn generous of you,'' and waving his hand at the men behind him, he asked, ''What you figure these boys are? Fence posts?''

''They look about as dumb as an oak post,'' Vent said, his eyes still cold and distant.

Looking at the sheriff, Bright asked, ''You pay this gent enough so he can afford to arrange his own funeral?''

"He don't work for me," Paley said.

"Neither do I," Carroll Rose said. He had stepped from an alley thirty feet behind the Circle-A riders and now he stood in the dust of the street, hands on hips, smiling at Canefield Bright.

Jerking his horse around, Bright stared at Rose, then snapped, "You're a dead man, Rose. A dead man . . ."

"You fixing to kill me?" Rose asked in his soft Texas drawl.

"If he does, I'm gonna plant a blue whistler right between his shoulder blades," Denton Rose said from a second-story window of the hotel across the street.

Bright, whose hand was inches from his gun, stiffened and then craned his neck around to stare at the older Rose, who was sighting down the barrel of a Winchester, its sights dead center on Bright's back.

"Best give it up," Paley advised softly.

"If you don't, you'll never leave this street standing up," Vent added.

"You couldn't beat me the best day you ever lived," Carroll Rose told him.

Looking at Vent, Bright said resignedly, "You'd be Leatherhand?"

At the name, the sheriff turned and stared at Vent and said softly, "And I'm the damn fool who insulted him."

"I know when I've got the losing hand," Bright admitted, and turning, he rode past Rose without looking at him, his shoulders stiff and his face taught with disappointment. His men trailed after him and as each man passed Rose, he looked down into the smiling face, then hastily looked away.

Nobody moved until Bright rode from sight around a distant bend of the twisty main street, then Rose looked up to where his father still cradled the rifle and said, "If you'll come down from there, I'll buy you a drink."

The rifle was pulled in and a few moments later, Denton Rose walked from the hotel and crossed the street. Carroll turned to Vent and asked, "You care to join us, Mr. Torrey?"

Looking at the sheriff and Paley, Vent said, "Come along, gentlemen, the well-heeled Mr. Rose is going to buy us a drink."

Denton went in the office and brought Carroll's coat to him and said, "The only reason I'm doing this is because I know you keep your money in your coat," and they crossed the street to the saloon.

Vent led the group into a saloon where they took a back table and ordered a bottle of whiskey. Evers gazed into his glass for a long time, then looked up at Vent and said, "Much obliged, Mr. Torrey, for backing my play out there. I reckon if you boys hadn't bought chips in that little game, I'd now be a memory."

Carroll Rose looked up and asked, "You got a family, Mr. Evers?"

Evers glanced at him and nodded.

Smiling his eternal smile, young Rose observed, "A feller that takes the chances you do maybe should outa get him some kinda insurance so his family won't starve after he goes under."

Paley smiled and then suddenly said, "Come on out back, boys. I want to show you something," and he rose and led them out the back door and, walking to a large pile of old cans and other trash, he selected ten bean cans and carefully lined them up against a dirt bank about fifty feet from the back of the saloon. Turning then, he stuck his head inside and called, "Ed, we're fixing to do a little target practicing,'' and then turned and nodding at Evers, said, ''Let her flicker, Dance.''

The sheriff suddenly went into a crouch and both guns appeared in his hands as if by magic, and in a thundering roll of gun shots spaced so close together they almost sounded as one, he put a bullet through each can.

Vent looked at the Roses, then grinned. ''Just goes to show you, boys, every feller who gets duded up ain't no plumb greenhorn,'' and he turned and went back into the saloon.

When they were all sitting down again, Evers looked at Vent then Carroll Rose and said quietly, ''Hell, I know I ain't in you fellers' bailiwick when it comes to using a six, but I reckon I'm good enough to take care of Lincoln County.''

''I'd say you're some better,'' Vent observed.

''Why the fancy clothes?'' Denton Rose asked.

The sheriff smiled. ''Throws a man off. He figures I'm just some flash gunman who climbed off yesterday's stage from the east. Hell, I was raised up in Montana on my daddy's stock ranch. Cut my teeth on a six . . .''

''What happened when you rode out to Spence's place?'' Paley asked curiously.

Evers grinned for the first time and it changed his whole appearance. No longer was he the blustering dandified pseudo-lawman. Instead, he was a pleasant-looking man with laugh wrinkles around his eyes. Staring at him, Vent marveled. He's like a damned chameleon, he thought as the sheriff said, ''Oh, old man Jordan looked at me as if I'd just crawled from under a rock, then his gunslick, Mick O'Reilly, he up and threw down on me and told me to take my warrant and go to hell. Old Spence, he accused me of being on the take . . .''

''Well, ain't you?'' Paley asked.

Unabashedly, Evers confessed, "Sure. Hell, it's a tradition here in Pioche. We've never had a sheriff in Lincoln County who didn't retire rich."

"Well, I'll be damned!" Carroll Rose exclaimed, staring at the sheriff as if he was seeing him for the first time.

Glancing at the gunman, Evers asked, "Mr. Rose, when you sit down at a poker table, do you always play the game square?"

Carroll glanced at his father and shrugged. "Got me there," he admitted.

Evers moved his eyes to Denton Rose and asked, "Mr. Rose, having been a rancher most of your life, I reckon you've traded a lot of horses. Ever fox a feller in a horse swap?"

Rose looked away, cleared his throat, started to answer, then said nothing. Turning to Paley now, Evers observed, "You work on a quota here in town, that right, Port?"

Port, seeing where he was going, said, "All right, Dance. You've made your point. Thievery is merely a matter of degrees. You just take more than the next feller," and he chuckled and shook his head.

Vent, listening to the sheriff's line of reasoning, suddenly realized he himself was cheating. I'm stealing time from my life, he thought and knew he had to get away from these men for a while. Standing up abruptly, he nodded, said, "Gonna check on my horse," and walked out.

Carroll Rose looked after him, the smile still on his face, his mad eyes glittering.

Vent walked along to the livery and saddled the Appy, mounted, and rode down canyon. Half an hour later he put the horse to a slope leading to a plateau and let him have his head as the powerful animal carried him to the top. Sitting there, allowing the horse to blow, he had his look at the country and then rode to a big rock, swung down, dropped the reins and, went and sat on its edge.

Thinking about Carroll and Denton Rose he wondered what would become of them. Denton had told Vent the boy was beyond bringing home. "Hell, he'd be in a shootout in a week back in Texas. Too many hotheads around. If he stayed there, somebody would eventually shoot him in the back."

Vent had looked him directly in the eye and said softly, "Denton, you know the boy's sick, don't you?"

Denton had looked away for a long moment and Vent thought he wasn't going to answer, then he met Vent's eyes and said softly, "I know. His mother was kinda strange too. I've lost him, Vent, and I'll never get him back this side of the grave. He's killed too many men and made too many enemies. They'll keep coming . . . Hell, you know about that . . ."

Vent knew about it. He had been forced to kill half a dozen men whose brothers, sons, or fathers had gone down before his guns. Each time he had tried to talk them out of going to the gun, but they would have it no other way. They were the ones who brought him the nightmares because he had no quarrel with them. They died because they felt honor bound to avenge their kin. Looking south toward the mining town of Panaca, he wondered if humans would ever learn.

Denton had told Vent he was going back to Texas. "Maybe I'll get me a little spread somewhere. Just a one-blanket outfit. Raise a few cows and some good horses. That way, if Carroll ever needs a place to come to, it'll be waiting," and listening to him, to the soft Texas drawl, Vent knew the old man was dreaming, that he knew in his heart his son would never ride back, that the only way the boy would come home was in a pine box aboard some baggage car with a tag hanging from a nail head.

Hating his thoughts, Vent rose and mounted the Appaloosa. Looking down at the big animal, he said softly, "You, old feller, you're the one thing that has never changed in my life," and the horse flicked its ears and then Vent rode him down the slope.

Paley sat on the veranda of Spence's ranch house and looked at the gaggle of riders sitting around the front yard and moving in and out of the bunkhouse and observed, "Sooner or later, Mr. Jordan, you're gonna have to do something with them boys."

Looking hard at Paley, Jordan finally asked, "What you suggest?"

"Let some of them go back to your ranch. Hell, you don't need that army."

Jordan thought a moment then said, "Paley, would Carroll Rose and Vent Torrey work for me?"

Paley took his time thinking about it, then said positively, "Rose might, but Vent Torrey? Never . . ."

"Why not? Hell, he likes money don't he?"

"He has never hired his gun and I don't see him doing it now, especially to a man who sent a bunch of gunmen after him," Paley declared.

"There is that," Jordan admitted.

"More like, he'll come looking for you . . ."

"I figured that, too," Jordan answered and then Mick O'Reilly came from the bunkhouse and sat on the front steps and, looking up at Jordan, asked, "Reckon you could talk this here limb of the law into taking a short trip up in the hills. They tell me the hunting and fishing up there is fine."

Jordan stared at him. "You got a plan working?"

"Just a thought," O'Reilly said.

Looking at Paley, Jordan asked, "What about it, marshal? You go fishing and when you come back, we'll all be gone."

"Who pays for burying the dead?" Paley asked.

"Hell, I'll foot the bill," Jordan replied, a frosty grin on his face.

"What about the sheriff?" Paley asked.

"That dude. Hell, he ain't gonna cause anybody trouble."

"Mr. Jordan, you ever have a horse that was real pretty and acted dead gentle all the time, then, when he got you just right, he exploded in seven different directions?"

"You're saying Evers is a sleeper?" Jordan asked and it was obvious he didn't believe Paley.

Looking Jordan straight in the face, Paley said quietly, "He can spot your man there a good second and beat him six outa six."

O'Reilly turned his head and stared at Paley, then asked, "What about you, marshal? Would you test his wind?"

Paley shook his head. "Not unless I had no other way to go and if I was in that kind of wrench, I'd order up a grave plot and casket before I braced him."

"Well I'll be damned," Jordan said.

"You ever see pictures of Wild Bill Hickok?" Paley asked.

"Hell, I saw old Wild Bill hisself once," Jordan declared.

"Notice how he dressed? Wore them fancy guns that looked as if he lifted them offa some Mex down in Juarez. Had a red sash wrapped around his belly . . . and that long cape with the checkers inside and the long hair that made him look like a girl. Pretty tony rigout, I'd say."

"You're right enough there," Jordan agreed.

"Then they's old General Custer. He was so damned

vain, he had his own uniforms designed. And those fancy
buckskin outfits made outa chewed deer hide . . .''

Jordan held up his hand. "You've made your point so
why don't you just take Evers with you on that hunting
trip?"

Paley thought about it, then looking coldly at Jordan,
said, "I'll go along with you, Mr. Jordan, but if you kill
or injure one damn citizen of Pioche or this county, I'll
personally whip the horse out from under you. You
understand?"

O'Reilly, sensing the deadly menace in Paley's voice,
looked at him sharply, then dropped his hand to his gun
and the marshal, staring at the hand, said softly, "When I
took the job of marshal in Pioche, they were planting a
man a week. Bitters and The Kid were the first men killed
in my town in over a year. Folks didn't just all at once
haul off and get religion. You follow me, Mr. O'Reilly?"

O'Reilly looked at Jordan and asked, "You want me to
put this peckerwood down, Mr. Jordan?"

Before Jordan could answer, Paley asked softly, "You
just born stupid, or do you have to work at it?"

O'Reilly's eyes suddenly flared and Paley knew he was
going for his gun and the marshal's hand slashed down and
up and the Frontier Colt's hammer clicked back, sending
O'Reilly an invitation to die. His gun was still in the
holster although he had begun his draw.

"Make it or break it," Paley challenged him.

Jordan raised a hand and said sharply, "Mick, leave it
be," and the Irishman let the gun drop back in leather and
said mildly, "Your some shuckins with that pistolo, mister
marshal."

Paley grinned and let the hammer down, reholstered the
gun and rose and walked down the steps past O'Reilly and
out to his horse and, mounting, turned and smiled and

said, "Tell Spence I'll fetch him some venison," and rode toward town.

O'Reilly looked across the yard, his gaze blank, then said quietly, "I reckon I'm getting too damn old for this game. Hell, I can't even read a man's pedigree anymore."

Chapter Seven

It was Monday morning and Pioche had just shaken off the cobwebs of night and risen to face the rising sun and a new day. Vent and Carroll Rose sat on the hotel veranda, the hot cups of coffee in their hands sending up a faint trail of steam as they quietly watched the street. In a room above them, Denton Rose had just put foot to the floor and was trying to touch the ceiling in a gigantic yawn, hands above his head, when he heard the sound of several horses approaching. Walking to the window, he gazed north and around a bend in Main Street, Elam Jordan, sided by Whitey Beard, Mick O'Reilly, Jeff Kidder, and three other Barbed-T riders, were coming into town at a trot. Knowing Vent and Carroll were just below him on the veranda, he thrust his head out the window and called, "Heads up, the Barbed-T coming in."

Vent looked at Carroll and said, "Time to take a little ride," and led the young gunfighter down an alley and north behind the business houses toward the livery. As they walked along the narrow alley, they met and passed the town's denizens just beginning the day's work. A cook from one of the many restaurants came to the door and threw out a pan full of dirty water, grinned at them, and said hello. A saloon swamper pushed his sweepings from a back porch where they fell to a pile from past cleaning efforts. A whore sat on a porch stoop and sleepily drank her morning coffee. Looking up, she smiled from a ravaged face, and said, "Morning, boys. Be open for business in another hour."

Carroll grinned at Vent and stopping for a moment, looked at the girl, then asked, "How come you're up so early, darlin'?"

"Guilty conscience, handsome," she replied, a mischievous grin on her lips.

"Ahhhh . . . ," Rose nodded and followed Vent on down the alley where they entered the back door of the stable and, quickly saddling the horses, rode out the back way and turned into the low hills to the west of town.

Back at the hotel, Denton Rose pulled up a chair and, sitting by the window where he had a clear view of the street, laid out his gun cleaning equipment and went to work on his .45.

Elam Jordan rode along the main street, his eyes flicking to right and left as he made his way to the doctor's office. Pulling in there, he turned to Beard and, pointing south, said, "Go down to that stable and see about a buggy. We're gonna take Powers and Hall back out to Spence's if the doc says they can travel," and not waiting for an answer, went inside.

Ten minutes went by and Jordan stuck his head out the door and ordered, "You, Harley, go tell Whitey to bring up the rig."

By the time Beard arrived at the doctor's office with the buggy, Jordan had Powers and Hall sitting on a bench in front of the place. Hall could only hobble and Powers carried his arm in a sling, but they were able to move around and the doctor had allowed them to leave, but warned Jordan they still needed a lot of rest. Beard and Kidder helped the two men into the buggy, handing the reins to Hall. Both Hall and Powers carried their handguns.

Jordan looked at the little doctor and said, "Doctor, the Barbed-T appreciates what you've done for these boys," and then he paid the medico and strode into the street, mounted his horse, and rode north.

As they passed the hotel, Jordan glanced up, saw Denton Rose sitting in the window, and pulled in his horse. Looking up at the ex-rancher, he said, "Mr. Rose, I thank you for your help. The Barbed-T is going home," and he waved and gigged up his horse.

Rose strapped on his gun, picked up his rifle, and went downstairs and out the back door, following the same route to the stables Vent and his son had taken.

Jordan was almost to the Dexter Stables when the first shot was fired. The bullet struck Mick O'Reilly in the stomach, folding him over the saddle horn. Then the street erupted into a roll of gun thunder as Canefield Bright and his men burst from alleys and doorways, guns fisted and blazing. Whitey Beard shot a Circle-A rider through the chest and watched him fall into a water trough, where his blood turned its contents an ugly brown. Jordan fired at Bright, missed and, jumping his horse into an alley, cursed wildly and shot a man who was standing in a saloon doorway firing a rifle. He had unloaded two Barbed-T saddles and the riders lay sprawled in the dust of the street. Beard rode to O'Reilly's assistance as the gunman started to slip from his horse and then two Bright riders ran into the street and fired point blank at him and Beard took both rounds in the chest and died before he hit the ground. O'Reilly, clinging grimly to his saddle horn, lifted his gun and shot one of them only to take a bullet through the left eye from the other. As the huge slug tore through his brain, he screamed in dying agony and somersaulted over the cantleboard of his saddle to crash into the dust.

Somehow, Jeff Kidder had managed to weather the hail of lead and now he was down in the street, his Winchester spewing lead as he held it hot against his leg and fired at anything that moved. Bright, trying to get a clear shot at Jordan, got nicked by one of Kidder's slugs, cursed wildly, and turned and shot the young rider through the throat, dropping him in the street. Kidder, game to the last, rolled over and cuddling the rifle to his shoulder, put a bullet in another Circle-A puncher as Bright, forgetting Jordan for the moment, rode right over top of him, firing a bullet into his back as he passed. The projectile ripped into the rider's spine, killing him instantly.

A bullet had dropped the buggy horse when the fight began and Powers and Hall, caught in the open conveyance, had drawn their guns and joined the fray. Now Hall, gripping his pistol two-handed, took careful aim and shot a Bright rider from the saddle. As the man fell, Bright whirled and shot twice very rapidly and Hall, struck in the chest and stomach, fell from the stalled buggy and died in the dirt. Powers, screaming curses, shot twice at Bright. His first slug struck the man's saddle horn and whined away viciously to rip through the front window of the barber shop, cascading its glass onto the sidewalk and driving the barber, who had been crouched by the door watching the fight, deeper into his shop. Then a Circle-A puncher, kneeling behind a water trough, carefully sighted on Powers' chest with his Winchester and shot him. The force of the slug whipped him backwards from the buggy and he landed in a sprawl on top of Hall, where he feebly tried to raise his gun, then, still cursing, died.

Whirling his horse, Bright lifted his gun and centered it on Jordan, who was frantically trying to reload his own smoking six.

"Leave it alone," Bright ordered coldly, and Jordan looked up and stared down the barrel of Bright's gun and let his own fall into the dust.

While two of Bright's men sat their horses guarding Jordan, Bright supervised the loading of his dead. There were no wounded.

Leading the bullet-marked cavalcade south from the town, he left the Barbed-T riders where they lay, pausing only long enough to spit a mouthful of tobacco juice into Mick O'Reilly's dead face.

Two miles from town Bright pulled rein and, glancing at Jordan, told two of his men, "Take this old has-been on east until you're pretty well away from where people might see you and put a bullet into his head."

Jordan said nothing, seemingly in shock as he sat slumped in the saddle. One of the riders leaned over and took Jordan's reins from him and led his horse east. Bright rode on, not bothering to look back.

Vent and Carroll Rose heard the riders approaching long before they arrived at the bottom of the little draw. "Looks like old Jordan done lost the waltz contest," Rose observed.

Then the little cavalcade drew rein and one of the riders said, "I reckon this is far enough," and looked at Jordan and said, "Hell, old man, you've had a good life. Now it's time for you to shuffle off. We'll bury you deep so the buzzards and the coyotes don't tear your carcass to pieces. How's that?"

Jordan didn't answer. It was as if he rode in a coma. Glancing at Rose, Vent said quietly, "Wait," and hurried down the gentle slope behind their position, quickly mounted the Appaloosa and rode around the point, dropped down into the canyon, and was thirty feet from the Circle-A riders and their intended victim before they were aware they had company.

"Howdy, boys," Vent saluted them. Then looking at Jordan, he said, "Well, well, what we got here. Looks like you boys done caught the old bull of the woods. What you fixing to do? Plug him?"

"What we do with this old hellion's none of your business, feller," one of the men said. Although both Circle-A riders had been in Pioche the day Vent and Carroll Rose had sided the sheriff, the men failed to recognize him.

Looking at the gunman, Vent asked, "What's your name, friend?"

Staring at Vent, who was staring back for all the world like a rattlesnake who has mesmerized a bird, the man said uncomfortably, "That ain't your put in. You'd best ride away from here while you still can," and he began to turn the naked gun in his hand.

Vent suddenly smiled and, drawing like broken chain lightning, shot the right-hand rider through the stomach, driving him over the shoulder of his horse, and then put a bullet into the second man, who grunted, clutched his chest, and swayed in the saddle, desperately trying to raise his gun into firing position. Cold-bloodedly, Vent took careful aim and slammed a second slug through the puncher's forehead, blasting the top of his head into his hat. It sailed from his head to bounce down the draw and slide to rest against a tumbleweed plant. Vent's third shot struck the wounded Circle-A rider half an inch to the right of his left shirt pocket, driving another grunt from him and knocking him into the dirt. Rolling over, the man stared up at Vent, his face a study in agony, and gasped, "Who . . . the . . . hell are . . . you?"

"Folks call me Leatherhand," he said and watched the man heave up a mouthful of blood and die.

Looking up into Jordan's eyes, Vent said softly, "So, Mr. Jordan, we meet at last."

Jordan, jarred back to reality by the rolling gun thunder, stared down at his two would-be killers and then up at Vent and shook his head. "They said you were good. I'll certify to that."

Looking at the two dead men, Vent said, "Them boys was just a bit hard to kill. Saw a dog that way once. Feller took him out to kill him 'cause he was sick. Took five .45s before he stopped kicking."

"Now what, Mr. Torrey?" Jordan asked.

"If I was him, I'd just up and hang you, Mr. Jordan," Carroll Rose said as he stood up on the bank and looked down at the rancher.

Vent smiled grimly and shook his head. "Don't think much of stretching a man's neck. Hard way to go. Rather just shoot him . . . . What happened in town, Mr. Jordan?"

"Bright, he caught us flat-footed. Killed them all . . ."

Vent stared at him. "You trying to tell me they wiped out the whole Barbed-T?"

"No, I left most of the boys at Ira Spence's ranch over in Clover Valley," Jordan explained. "Took Whitey, O'Reilly, and Kidder along and three other boys; Harley Polk, Bert Darling, and Tex Dalton. They're all dead. So's Powers and Hall. We come to take them back to Spence's. Was going back home. Bright hit us from cover. We didn't have a damn chance."

Carroll Rose rode up then and nodding at Jordan, said, "Take it Mr. Torrey doesn't believe in an eye for an eye."

Vent quickly filled Rose in and then said, "Let's swing

around town and head for Clover Valley. It may come as some surprise to Mr. Bright that his boys didn't get the job done.''

Jordan sat on his horse for a moment in silence, then looking Vent square in the eye, said quietly, ''It appears, Mr. Torrey, I made one hell of a bad call on you. Half my outfit's dead and Bright's won the first round. Now you come along and save my bacon for me. I owe you more than I can pay, but I never forget a favor.''

Vent answered just as quietly. ''Mr. Jordan, long after this is over and folks have almost forgotten it, them that do recall will lay the blame on your doorstep. I reckon that's enough for any man to live with. . . . They's a lot of good men in Boot Hill because of your bad judgment. That you'll also have to live with. Let's ride,'' and he turned and led them up and out of the draw. As they topped out, the distant slam of a Sharps buffalo gun sent its echoes across the sprawling land in waves of sound.

Vent had been looking back at Jordan when the shot was fired and now he watched as the old man swayed in the saddle, groaned and lifted a hand in a futile gesture to paw his bullet-punctured chest, then blood gushed from his open mouth and he slid from the saddle. As he hit the ground, Vent and Rose slammed the guthooks to their horses and swerved opposite directions, riding in a wide circle and breaking over a low ridge in a dead heat, where they caught a man in a high Mexican sombréro desperately trying to mount his skittish horse. Lifting his .44, Vent shot the bushwacker in the side and watched him spin away and collapse in the buffalo grass, his rifle still in its scabbard on the horse. As he fell, the animal bolted away and Vent called, ''Pick up the pony, Carroll,'' and rode down on the wounded man as he tried to crawl away through the brush and high grass. When Vent slid to a stop above him, the man feebly pawed at his gun, then rolled over and, lying on his back, looked up at Vent and said, "Ah, to hell with it," and let his hand fall away from his gun butt.

Vent dismounted and jerking the man's pistol from its holster, tossed it to one side. He was squatting on his heels looking at the bushwacker when Rose rode up, the runaway horse in tow. Sliding to a stop, he looked down at the man and said, "Ain't dead, huh?"

"Not yet," Vent answered, then asked the wounded man, "Who sent you, pard?"

"Go jump a sheep," the man said weakly.

Vent looked up at Rose and observed, "This old boy's got a lot of hard bark on him, ain't he?"

" 'Peers that way," Rose agreed laconically, then added, "Don't reckon he'll impress old St. Pete much though."

"If you don't loosen up that tongue, I'm gonna set fire to one of these creosote bushes and toss your carcass on top, seeing as they ain't much in the way of wood around here."

"Now . . . why in the . . . hell would a man . . . do that?" the wounded man asked feebly, his eyes starting to grow dim.

"Because he's a mean son-of-a-bitch," Rose volunteered.

"What the hell . . . Bright gave me the orders. Said . . . I should . . . trail along . . . just in case . . . old Jordan bought . . . our boys off . . . was to plant a blue whistler . . . in him . . . . Did it. Old man's dead . . ."

Looking up at Rose, Vent said, "I'll hang around here for a little bit if you'll go fetch the old man."

Wordlessly, Rose turned his horse and, trailing the bushwacher's mount, rode over the ridge. When he returned leading Jordan's horse with the old man's body slung over the saddle horn, he found Vent mounted and ready to ride. The bushwacker was dead.

Looking at Rose, he said, "He died game."

They rode into Spence's front yard half an hour after Stalls had returned carrying the Barbed-T dead hanging from their horses. Denton Rose had rode the bottom from his horse in an attempt to reach Stalls and let him know what was happening in town. Now the men carefully unloaded the bullet-riddled bodies of their friends and laid them out along the corral. When Stalls looked up and saw Vent and Carroll Rose approaching, carrying the old man slung over the saddle, he walked out and had his look and said, "How?"

"Two fellers rode him out into the brush country. Bright ordered it. I sorta stepped in and sent them off to play harps. We was heading back here when a gent with a Sharps punched your boss's ticket. I killed the bushwacker."

Nodding, Stalls led the horse over to the corral and untied its grisly burden. Lowering the old man, he laid him out at the head of the column of the dead and stood staring down into his face.

"You and Bright are going to be playing a harp duet right damn soon," Stalls promised, then tolling off six men, had them begin digging graves in the ranch graveyard. Vent climbed the steps and sat down beside Ira Spence and said quietly, "Out there lies a monument to one man's stubbornness."

"Well, nobody paid any higher price for the privilege," Spence observed.

Canefield Bright sat against a large boulder and contemplated his next move while staring into the flames of a late-evening campfire. It was cold here on the edge of the desert after the sun went down and he wore a heavy Mackinaw and wished he was back in Louisiana where the worst they had to contend with was rain. But he knew he would not leave until Carroll Rose was in his grave if it meant killing the boy's father and even Leatherhand.

Leatherhand; an enigma to Canefield Bright. What made a man like that tick? What did he live for? He was a gambler, so folks said, but he gambled in moderation. He did not consort with saloon girls and if he had a woman somewhere, he kept it a secret. His gun was not for hire, yet men said he was faster than Bill Longley, Bill Hickok, Wes Hardin, Doc Holiday, and even Carroll Rose, a man he himself had seen in terrible action.

Thinking back on that day in the saloon at Cedar City, he still marveled that any man could be so fast. He was no slouch with a gun, but young Rose was magic. And then Bright thought, if he is so fast and Leatherhand can beat him, how fast is Leatherhand? He decided he was not going to try and find out. I'll just plug the son-of-a-bitches in the back, he thought.

Crimp Blair came from supervising the care of their horses and, squatting in front of the fire, looked up at his boss and observed, "Nights sure as hell get cold in this country."

Blair had been ramrod of the Circle-A for ten years and had taken more than one Circle-A herd north to sell to the Yankees. He had a mean reputation in Louisiana and east Texas for being quick on the trigger, but looking at him now, Bright realized he was no match for the likes of Vent Torrey or Carroll Rose.

"Riders coming in," one of the Circle-A punchers called.

Bright and Blair rose and stood waiting as two horsemen pulled up just beyond the camp and one of them inquired, "All right if we come in?"

"Come ahead," Bright invited and watched Port Paley and Dance Evers ride up to the edge of the light and sit waiting for an invitation to dismount.

"Climb down, boys, and rest your saddles," Bright said and the two lawmen dismounted and came to the fire. Watching them, Bright sensed a change in Evers. Gone was the bluster, and gone were the fancy clothes. Instead, he was dressed in Levis and chaps and a battered, rain-crimped Stetson. Unless a man knew who he was, they would take him for just another puncher or grubliner.

Walking to the fire, the sheriff looked at Bright and observed, "Figured you boys would be halfway back to Louisiana by now."

"Got a little unfinished business here first," Bright said casually.

"Like bumping off Carroll Rose?" Paley asked.

"Something like that," Bright nodded.

"Got a little news for you," Evers smiled. "Those two Circle-A waddies you sent Jordan off with . . . well, they kinda met with a sudden accident. However, Mr. Bright, the bushwhacker you sent to back them up did his job; he put the old man down. He wound up going to help them other two boys . . . wherever they went . . ."

Bright stared at him. "Who killed them?"

Smiling, Evers answered, "Damn if I know, but it was Torrey and young Rose who brought the old man's body in to Ira Spence's place."

"So . . ."

"I reckon," Evers agreed.

Paley looked at Bright and said quietly, "Mr. Bright, you and your men killed several fellers in the streets of Pioche. Now I don't know the right of that because I wasn't in town then, but even in my town we hold coroner's inquests. Our citizens don't take kindly to murder in the streets no matter who commits it. Bad for business. Now, my authority doesn't reach outside the town limits, but the sheriff's does and he has warrants for you and your men charging murder.''

Bright grinned. "That's interesting, Mister Marshal, but just how the hell are you going to serve them?''

Evers' eyes were cold as he said, "You got a choice, Mr. Bright. Either you come in peaceable or slung across your saddles. Personally, I don't cotton to you so I'd just as soon deliver your remains to the undertaker. Save the town the cost of good hemp to stretch your neck.''

Bright threw back his head and laughed loudly, then suddenly jerked his thumb toward where his men had gathered in a semi-circle around the outskirts of the fire. "Just what the hell do you two damn fools propose to do with my men?''

Glancing at them, Evers said off-handedly, "Ah hell, Mister Bright, we'll just tote them on in too, if they resist.''

Looking at Crimp Blair, Bright observed, "Tell me, Mr. Blair, have you ever seen anything like this?''

Blair, shaking his head, remarked, "I've been to two county fairs, a hog calling and a hanging and I ain't never seen its match. No sireee . . .''

Staring at Evers, Bright asked, "You fellers really figure to just waltz in here and arrest us and if we don't cave in and submit, you're gonna shoot us up?''

"That's right, mister," Evers said. "You don't shuck them guns and come along plumb docile, you're gonna be dead as a nit in about three seconds.''

"Well, Mister Sheriff, I hope you got an army with you 'cause you're gonna need it to take me and my boys to jail.''

"Funny you should mention an army," Evers mused, and then he turned his head and called, "Captain Bellows, will you come in here, please," and Bright turned and stared. A tall cavalry officer stepped into the light. As he walked toward the fire, the solid slam of breech bolts being locked on Spencer rifles came clearly to the men gathered there and they froze, their hands suddenly held wide of their guns.

"What the hell . . . ?" Bright muttered.

Removing a sheet of paper from an inside pocket, Evers calmly read the words of a warrant mandating the arrest of Bright and his men, then snapped, "Mr. Bright, order your men to drop their guns at their feet and step back, please."

Bright hesitated for a long moment, then turned and said, "You heard him, boys. Dump the hardware," and stood stolidly while his men unbuckled their guns and let them fall.

The cavalry officer turned and called "Corporal Jackson, detail two men to gather up these men's weapons, then saddle their horses and prepare to return to Pioche."

Nodding at the captain, Paley said, "Meet Captain Archer Bellows, Fifth Cavalry, United States Army."

"So you're from Louisiana, Mr. Bright," Bellows said. "I was there in the spring of sixty-two when Farragut forced New Orleans' surrender. Never cared much for it. Too much rain," and he smiled coldly.

Bright, staring at the officer, decided he would be very careful with this man. It was obvious he didn't like southerners, and particularly southerners from Louisiana.

They arrived in Pioche at midnight and Evers locked up Bright and his remaining ten men and left Thomas and the troops to guard them while he, Paley, and Bellows went across the street for a drink.

As they sat at a back table and sipped their whiskey, Evers said, "Captain, we here in Pioche appreciate this. We probably won't be able to make a murder charge stick, but we will put these fellers on record that Lincoln County is off limits to hardcases."

Bellows looked at Evers shrewdly, then asked, "Where were you boys when this shindig began?"

"Believe it or not, we had gone north to serve a damn tax summons and on the way back decided to do a little hunting," Evers said with a straight face.

"I heard from a couple of your citizens that Jordan wanted you men out of town so he'd have a clear shot at Bright," the captain noted. "Appears he was hoisted on his own lance, so to speak."

"Well, he won't make that mistake again," Evers said, then glanced up and breathed, "Oh, oh . . ."

Bellows looked across his shoulder and saw three men just entering the saloon. In the lead was a tall man with a young-old face. Dressed like any puncher in off the range, his only distinguishing mark was an odd leather glove on his gunhand. The man directly behind him wore gambler's black, set off by a white shirt and black string tie. He wore a .45 Colt on his hip. He also wore a peculiar cross-draw rig that placed the butt of a .44 Russian break-top even with his belt buckle. The third man had premature gray hair and a hard face that had seen its share of miles and troubles.

They stopped in front of the table and Evers said, "The he wolves of the West have come to visit us."

Half turning so he could keep an eye on the room, the boy in the gambler's rig smiled a beautific smile and said, "If this here feller wasn't the limb of the law around here, I'd put him under."

Jerking a thumb at the speaker, Paley said, "Captain Bellows, meet Carroll Rose. The gent with the funny glove is Vent Torrey and the white-maned hombre is the segundo of the Barbed-T, Cap Stalls."

Bellows looked at Rose and observed, "They tell me, Mr. Rose, you're the undertaker's best friend . . ."

The smile stayed on Rose's face.

The captain then turned his eyes to Vent and, taking his time, looked him over. When their eyes met, the captain was the first to look away.

Glancing at Stalls, Bellows said, "My condolances on the death of your employer, Mr. Stalls. He had a good reputation among officers of the cavalry. In fact, I myself have purchased remounts from him in the past and never had a complaint. He also furnished beef for a couple of the reservations where I was an officer. His count was always accurate and the beef in good shape. Folks will miss him."

Stalls looked at the floor, then said quietly, "Captain, Elam Jordan made his share of mistakes and God knows coming here was the biggest, but he was a hard man and a stubborn one. Once he bit into something, he did not cotton to spitting it out. It killed him and it killed some damn good men with him."

"Those who did the shooting are across the street in my jail," Paley said. "There'll be a coroner's inquest tomorrow and if the coroner decides it was murder, he'll convene a grand jury to hear the evidence. Meanwhile, the judge will set bail and I can promise you it'll be high."

"You figure you can keep him and that bunch of gun waddies of his in your jail?" Vent spoke for the first time. He had been standing with his back against the wall, listening quietly.

Paley looked up at him and replied, "All we can do is try."

"That's all a steer can do," Vent smiled.

Bellows rose and nodding at the assembled men, said, "I've done all I have time to do, Sheriff, now I've got to

be moving east. Injun trouble over on the border,'' and he
saluted and walked out.

"We kinda recruited the Army to help us bring Bright
in,'' Evers said.

"Who you got guarding the prisoners?'' Vent asked.

"Thomas. He's over there right now,'' Paley replied.

"It'll take more than that,'' Rose told him.

"Reckon you're right,'' Paley agreed and rose and went
out.

As Vent turned to Rose, a shuddering roar of guns from
the street galvanized the three men at the table into instant
action. Vent hit the door in a long shallow dive, driving it
aside with his shoulder and landing in a crouch on the
sidewalk, gun up and seeking a target. Flame lanced and
danced from an alley, seeking him out and he lifted the .44
and fired, heard a shout and knew he had scored.

Evers burst from the saloon behind him and now he
hunkered down behind a pile of grain bags in front of the
feed store next door to the saloon and guns at the ready,
stared across the street. Nothing moved over there in the
darkness and Vent asked Evers quietly, "Rose?''

"Out the back. He's circling,'' and then someone fired
from next door to the jail and the bullet smashed a window
behind Vent, ripping on into the interior of the saloon. He
heard it smash into the bottles on the backbar.

Evers fired instantly, but Vent couldn't tell whether he
hit a man or not.

"Who the hell's over there?'' the sheriff growled.

"I reckon Bright and his boys done broke jail,'' Vent
guessed and then someone fired from somewhere near
Dexter's Livery and Evers cursed as the bullet struck a
copper-bottomed tub near him and sang viciously over his
head.

"Them fellers mean business,'' he said and answered

the shot. His reward was the scream of a horse and then they heard the animal fall heavily and begin thrashing in the street down there somewhere and Evers observed, ''Probably find out it's my own damn horse,'' and fired again.

Vent was grateful he and Rose had left their horses at the stable on the south end of town as he searched the darkness for movement.

Suddenly gun roar cascaded its echoes along the narrow twists of Main Street and Vent looked north and saw the stabs of flame marking the shooters and thought, Rose has got behind them, and hoped the smiling gunfighter would drive whoever it was back toward the jail.

''I'm going to cross over,'' Evers said and before Vent could protest, he was up and running obliquely across the street, aiming for a doorway just south of the jail. He was halfway across when a long streak of fire backed by the solid slam of a .45 reached out and tagged him. Vent heard the bullet strike and thought, damn, that reached pay dirt, and then saw Evers pitch onto his face in the dust. As the Missourian squinted into the darkness, he could just make out the dark outline of Evers heavy body and ten feet from it another body. Hoping he was wrong, Vent surmised the second man was Port Paley.

To hell with it, he thought and came up fast and ran south along the sidewalk, his .44 pointing across the street. He was thirty feet from the saloon when the first shot came. He heard its intimate whisper of death as it fanned past his cheek and dodged into a doorway, letting loose three shots so closely spaced, they sounded as one. This time he knew he scored for he saw a dark shadow suddenly reel from the saddle shop doorway and stumble into the street, where the man stood and muttered, ''Ah God, I'm hit,'' and Vent lifted his gun and ruthlessly cut him down.

"That you, Milt?" a voice called from south of him and Vent, reloading, whispered, "Hell yes. Keep your voice down," and watched as the man detached himself from the shadows and came cat-footing along the sidewalk. Lifting the reloaded .44, Vent cooly slammed a bullet into the man's chest and heard him grunt and fall heavily.

There was a long silence, then the Bright man whined, "Milt, you shot . . . me," and Vent heard his groan and the rattle of his final breath leaving his lungs and knew Bright was another man down.

Two more shots came from up near the livery and Vent thought, they're trying to reach their horses and Carroll's got them cut off, and ran north, keeping tight in against the buildings. No one shot at him. When he reached the corner south of the stables, he ran west until he came up against the beginnings of a slope and then turned north again and ran swiftly along behind the stables, seeing no one. When he hauled up behind the place, he froze against the outside wall, not wanting to become a target for Rose. Then he saw the ladder. It was nailed to the outside of the livery barn and led upward to the open door of the loft. Quietly putting boot to rung, he climbed toward the opening. He was almost there when he heard footsteps coming hurriedly along the alley, then two shadows came together directly below him and Vent, .44 in hand, held his breath as someone said, "We've got to get in there. Without them horses, we're boxed."

"If we don't get the hell outa Nevada, we'll all swing now," the second man declared.

Then they spotted the ladder.

As they lifted their eyes upward, Vent did not hesitate. He shot twice, scoring both times as one man screamed in awful agony and staggered away from the wall to collapse over a pile of rubbish. The second man, apparently not hit as hard, stumbled south toward the corner then turned and lifted his gun. Before he could trigger a shot the barn door whipped open and a dart of fire leaped from Rose's gun barrel and the man was knocked spinning along the side of the barn. He clung desperately to the wooden bats for a moment, then slid down the wall and laying his head against the side of the building, said distinctly, "You son-of-a-bitch," and died.

Rose looked up and Vent saw the quick gleam of his teeth and knew he was smiling.

Climbing down Vent went inside and closed the door. A lantern sent its dim glow along the center passage between the stalls and, glancing toward the stable office, he saw a tousled-haired man staring out at them.

"The stable swamper," Rose said.

Looking at the long line of horses in their stalls, Vent noted the stamping and rolling of eyes and said, "Them ponies is just a little spooked, ain't they?"

"They're all Circle-A broncs," Rose replied.

Vent had a sudden thought. "What would you do if you couldn't get in here?"

"I'd go where horses were . . . Damn! The other stables," Rose snapped and they dodged out the door and ran south behind the businesses, heading for the livery where both their horses were stalled. Reaching the north side of the barn, Vent whipped east along the alley while Rose ran on to the other corner. Just as he hit the street, Vent heard the sudden clatter of hooves and then six riders burst from the stable door and Vent recognized the Appaloosa and lifted his gun and emptied the big horse's saddle, then whistled shrilly and watched as the horse wheeled and ran back toward him.

The Circle-A hand who had stolen Rose's horse didn't have much better luck for the big animal suddenly bogged

its head and went into a wild, twisting bucking spree that
ended with the rider hurled from its back and through a
large window fronting a haberdashery store.

Rose came up to Vent, smiled his wild smile, and said,
"One-man horse," and ran across the street with Vent
close behind him. The thrown rider was just clambering
from the window holding his arm and the way it hung
loosely down his side, Vent figured it was broken. Rose
calmly jerked his gun from its holster and tucked it behind
his own belt, then said harshly, "Walk, neighbor."

When they reached the jail, they found two dozen townsmen gathered around the bodies of Paley and the sheriff.
One of the men looked up, saw their prisoner, and said
bitterly, "Here's one of the bastards who did for Port and
Dance. Get a goddamned rope."

Vent looked at Rose and then shrugged and turned away
as the townsmen moved in. Watching them drag the man
toward the shipping pens and a high arched gate, Vent
observed, "Normally I'd put a stop to that. Don't hold
with lynching, but this is their town and their lawmen are
dead. Let's get your paw and ride the hell outa here."

Chapter Eight

Vent led his tired men into Shakespeare, New Mexico, almost a month to the day that Canefield Bright had broke from the Pioche jail. During that time, Bright, cut down by the Pioche fight to five men, including Crimp Blair, had led his pursuers up and down Arizona from Phoenix to Jerome; over the slopes of Mingus Mountain, and then east into New Mexico, where they paused briefly at Lincoln to resupply. From there Bright doubled back and rode west almost to the Nevada border. Vent had followed the tracks of Bright's horses for so long he could shut his eyes and see them perfectly. He knew he would recognize them if he saw them five years from then. Now those tracks led to the outskirts of Shakespeare and then disappeared among the hundreds of other tracks leading to the town.

"Some burg," Carroll Rose noted, looking along the main street to where the sign STRATFORD HOTEL hung over the street.

"A tough town," Vent said and turned into the huge adobe corral next door to the hotel and dismounted. Looking at the ground in the dusty corral, Vent did not recognize any of the tracks as those they were following, but knew they could have come and gone and been stomped out by the animals that came here later.

"Help you fellers?" a man asked and Vent turned and looked at him and saw a tall fellow wearing bib overalls and carrying a manure fork.

"Need grain for these animals and a good rubdown. Want them watered slow. You got good hay?"

"It's fair," the man said, and looked curiously at Carroll Rose, whose long, golden hair and eternal smile made him a curiosity to most any man. When the stable hand's eyes dropped to the odd belly holster the younger Rose wore he looked away.

Watching this byplay, Denton Rose asked, "How much?" and the man, jarred back to the reality of paying customers, replied, "One dollar a horse and if you take rooms in the hotel, we knock off a quarter for each pony."

Glancing at the hostler, Carroll Rose cautioned, "If you're in the habit of riding stabled animals to water, best lead mine. He's a one-man horse and he can buck like a son-of-a-bitch."

Listening to young Rose's soft drawl, Vent began to understand why men made mistakes with him. He seemed on the surface little more than a happy-go-lucky Texan out for a lark and until aroused, his eyes gave away nothing, holding only bland innocence in their depths. Vent knew that when anger rode the youthful Texan, something came up in those eyes and peered madly out at the world and by then it was far too late. The look in the boy's eyes usually came at the moment he went for his gun. Now he glanced at Vent and asked, "Food, bed, or booze?"

Denton removed his hat and slapped the dust from it against a chap leg and said, "Me, I think I'll go register and wash off some of this trail dust. You fellers want me to get rooms for you?''

Carroll nodded and Vent, pulling his Winchester from its scabbard, handed it to Denton and said, ''Appreciate it. We'll be along after we've had a dust cutter or two,'' and he and Carroll left the stable.

Turning in at the Grant House Stage Station and Saloon, they stopped just inside to allow their eyes to adjust to the dimness of the room and then Vent saw Cap Stalls and what was left of the Barbed-T crew leaning against the long bar. Each man showed the stains of hard travel. Walking down the room, Vent stopped just behind Stalls and looking at him in the mirror, observed, ''A man who's trailing other men should maybe learn to grow eyes in the back of his head,'' and Stalls looked up, grinned and said softly, ''Bang, I'm dead,'' and turned and leaned his elbows against the bar.

''You're a long way from South Pass City, Cap,'' Vent said.

''Trying to find a killer,'' the segundo answered.

''Looks like you sent some of your boys home,'' Carroll Rose observed.

Looking at him, Stalls said, ''Four of my men took the old man home for burial and to see that things keep running on the ranch. We been trying to come up on Bright's bunch.''

''He's either here or he's been here,'' Vent said.

''He was here two days ago,'' Stalls informed them. ''I wired the marshal and he sent a wire back. Said Bright was in town, but that he couldn't arrest him. Didn't have a warrant.''

''Who's the marshal here now?'' Rose asked.

A big man pushed his way into the bar and, glancing at Rose, said, ''Move it, youngster, or I'll move it for you.''

Stalls grinned and nodding at the bartender, said, "Give this gent a drink. I figure he can use a sendoff."

The man turned a sour look on Stalls and asked, "You planning on sending me off, are you?"

Stalls shook his head. "Not me, neighbor. You didn't crowd me away from the bar . . . but you did shove Carroll Rose here to one side," and he watched the man's face slowly whiten as he looked at the now cold-eyed youth with the weird smile plastered on his face and the long-fingered hands caressing his gunbutt.

As the man backed away from the bar, he said hastily, "Sorry. I ain't no pistol fighter, Mr. Rose. Guess I was just feeling ornery. Had a knock down, drag out with the old woman this morning . . ."

The look faded from Rose's eyes just as a man wearing a star came in the back door, looked around and seeing Stalls, walked over and said, "Mr. Stalls, this feller Bright left town early this morning. Stable hand said he and his men rode outa here about five o'clock," then the marshal spotted Vent and grinned and stuck out his hand.

"Vent Torrey, by God," and Vent solemnly shook hands as every eye in the place turned toward the group at the bar.

"How are you, Rand?" Vent asked, surprised to see Rand Carpenter still the town's marshal.

"Fine as frog's hair," Carpenter said.

Holding up a finger Vent said, "Run that horse around the corral again, barkeep," and watched as the bartender poured glasses to the brim, then set out an extra for the marshal and filled it until the sour mash whiskey ran over the lip.

"Helgar still working for you?" Vent asked, remembering the wild-eyed deputy from his last visit to Shakespeare. He had been trailing a man then too and had found him in the lobby of the Shakespeare House. When the gunsmoke settled, three men were dead and Vent had retrieved $50,000 in stolen bank money.

Carpenter looked at the floor and said softly, "You know, that feller was as crazy as hell, but I sorta liked him. He took on four gents from Sante Fe who rode in here on the stage. There was warrants for all of them and that damned fool tried to serve them. They just naturally weighted him down with lead."

"Happens," Rose nodded, then Denton came in and walked to the bar and grinned when he saw Stalls, remarking, "The bad penny," and dropping a hand on his son's shoulder, asked, "Reckon it's about time you bought your paw a drink."

Nodding at the bartender, Rose turned as Vent said, "Rand, this here's Carroll Rose and his father, Denton," and watched the wariness he had come to expect creep into the marshal's eyes as he carefully shook hands with both men.

"You sure as hell travel with some high-class company," he observed, adding in an aside to Stalls, "The last time this gent hit town, his saddle pard was The Preacher and they shot hell outa the place. Left me three dead men to bury."

Then Vent caught a glimpse of movement at the top of a stairway leading to the second story of the sprawling hotel-stage station, and looked up, watching the small, compact figure in the dark gambler's clothes and twin guns descend. When he reached the main floor, he strolled over and stood in front of Vent and pushing his flat-crowned hat back from a mop of curly blonde hair, asked, "Where in hell have I seen you before?"

Looking solemn, Vent countered, "Damned if I know. What part of hell you come from?"

"You're in hell now, neighbor," the gambler said, then glancing at Carroll, smiled, nodded and observed, "Birds of a feather . . . How you, Mr. Rose?"

"Never been better, Mr. Monroe," Rose answered, then putting a hand on Denton's shoulder, said, "This here's my father, Denton Rose . . . from east Texas."

Gil Monroe shook hands, looked at Vent and then turned and asked Carpenter, "How come you allow these here grubliners to hang around our town?"

"Hell, you been here for four years," the marshal smiled.

Vent jerked a thumb at Stalls and said, "Meet Cap Stalls, segundo of the Barbed-T from over to South Pass City. Cap, this here's Gil Monroe, an honest gambler."

Monroe shook hands then asked innocently, "Looking for strays, Mr. Stalls?"

"You might call it that," Stalls countered.

"Funny thing," Monroe said thoughtfully, "Gent from Louisiana hit town couple days ago. Mean-looking jigger. Had guns stuck all over him. Figured if he fell down, he'd probably hurt himself. Five fellers with him. One of them was Crimp Blair. . . . Kinda knowed old Crimp in Virginia City when I was puddling around up there. Mighty quick man with a gun, as I recall."

"So they say," Stalls answered.

"You fellers had supper?" Carpenter asked.

"We was kinda thinking about it," Vent answered.

"Fine restaurant right across the street," the marshal said. "Hell, I'll join you. Ain't et yet either."

Monroe smiled. "His wife owns the place so he just kinda tries to round up a little trade for her."

Vent stared at him. "You got hitched?"

Carpenter smiled broadly. "Damn right. Ain't no reason why a city marshal cain't tie the knot."

"Was Helgar married?" Carroll asked.

"Yep . . . Now I'm married to his widow," Carpenter said and there was a twinkle in his eye.

Shaking his head Vent said, "Well, let's go see if she can cook, too," and led the way across the street, saying as he passed Monroe, "Come join us, Gil."

When they were seated on a bench against the wall with a ten-foot long table before them, Vent looked at Monroe and asked, "Heard The Preacher came through here some months back?"

Monroe nodded. "Me and him, we split a bottle and divided up the players at a three-card monte table and separated them from their cash. It was painless for them and profitable for us."

"Last I heard, he was over in Bodie with Arkie Chan," Vent said.

"Where's Owney Sharp now?"

"Holed up. Got plugged in Denver."

Monroe turned and looked at Vent and shook his head. "Damn shame. How bad?"

"He'll make her," Vent told him. Then Carpenter's wife came from the back room, walked to the table and, hands on hips, surveyed the group. "Hello, Mr. Monroe," she said, then looking pointedly at Carpenter, asked, "Ain't you ashamed of traveling with a feller like this here marshal?"

"It's sad," Monroe agreed. "Being reduced to hanging out with gents like him."

Then she boldly examined Vent, smiled at him, and turned to Carroll and stopped and stood staring as if she were seeing an apparition. Vent looked at the table and Denton gazed out the window. Monroe smiled faintly and Carpenter frowned.

Still staring at the youthful gunman, she asked, "What'll

it be boys? I got steaks fresh cut from the steer, backstrap from a deer Rand brought in three days ago, or you can have either stew or chili."

"The chili's so hot it would curl a Mex's hair," Carpenter told them and then added, "but that's the way I like it, so that's what I'll have."

"You got any money, mister?" his wife asked, wide-eyed. Looking at her, Vent could understand why the marshal married her. She was a big, buxom woman with hair as ripe as cornsilk and eyes that would melt the soul of an Apache scalphunter.

"Broke flatter than a pickpocket's victim," Carpenter said.

"Damn grubliners," his wife mumbled, then looked at the others and Vent ordered steak, potatoes, gravy and biscuits, and a gallon of coffee. Monroe asked for the stew and Stalls and his men ordered the deer steaks.

Looking at Carroll, the woman asked, "And you, sir?"

Smiling softly, Carroll said, "I'll have the steak," then glanced at Denton and the older man nodded, said, "That'll do fine," and she hesitated, then left hurriedly for the kitchen.

Vaguely Vent wondered what women saw in the smiling gunman, then figured it was probably the aura of violence and danger that seemed to exude from him.

Canefield Bright sat his horse on a hill overlooking the mining town of Shakespeare and watched the Lilliputian figures trudging along the streets in the early morning coolness on their way to the mines. Each man wore a hat with a holder for a candle on it and carried a lunch pail. Thinking about what it must be like to sit down 200 feet underground and calmly eat your lunch, he shook his head. The only way they're gonna get me underground is to plant me in a six-foot hole, he thought, then somberly wondered how long it would be before that happened. He had no illusions about what he and his men would face if caught before they crossed into Louisiana. He had watched Cap Stalls and his men ride into town the day before and he knew Stalls would kill him without mercy if he ever got his sights lined on him. He was far more worried about what Leatherhand and the two Roses were up to. Denton Rose he didn't concern himself with, but Carroll Rose was a skunk of another color. He had seen him in action and he wanted no part of that kind of game again. As for Leatherhand, they said he was even faster than young Rose and Bright wondered how that could be.

Thinking about home, he suddenly realized he wanted to return there very badly. The killing of Sheriff Evers and Marshal Paley had been a terrible error. It had outlawed them, and now they were on the run and until they reached Louisiana, would be fair game for any lawman's gun. Once back in their home state, Bright, one of the oldest names there, knew no governor would ever allow him to be extradited, nor would they turn him over to the law. He had friends in the legislature and the senate and one or two Brights had even been state senators and congressmen in the past. It was a proud name and his home state would not allow it to be dragged in the dirt by the courts of another jurisdiction.

Glancing back down at the now bustling town, he watched Stalls and his men leave a cafe on the main drag and walk to the livery, where they disappeared inside. When they emerged again, they were mounted and rode north. They'll cut our trail somewhere out there, Bright thought, and toyed with the idea of laying a trap for the Barbed-T and finishing the job he had started on the streets of Pioche.

Then Crimp Blair rode up the slope from where his men

were camped in a draw and stopping beside Bright, asked, "We move on this morning?"

Thinking about it, Bright suddenly made a decision. "No, I don't think so. The way we're going, they'll come up on us sooner or later. If Stalls' bunch don't manage to track us down, then Rose and Leatherhand will. That damned Vent Torrey tracks like an Injun. There ain't gonna be no losing him."

"So, what's our next move?"

"We're gonna split up and take separate trails outa here," Bright said. "We'll send a couple of the boys out on the stage; a couple more can ride south to the railroad and catch the train through Texas. That leaves you and me, Crimp."

"If those boys catch us, we'll stretch hemp," the gunman pointed out morosely.

Bright stared at him. "No damn Bright's ever been hanged and I ain't gonna break that record," he said harshly.

"Then how we gonna dodge those damn trackers?"

"You and I will separate here. You ride due east and I'll go due west. Once I'm clear of New Mexico, I'll head north into Wyoming and take the Immigrant Trail over South Pass. They'll never figure me for that. Hell, that's Elam Jordan's territory and me, I'm gonna ride right through it."

Blair didn't like it. He was too well known in this part of the country. His reluctance showed on his face and Bright, seeing it, said, "Look, once you're clear of the mining towns, you'll be fine. Just keep to the high ground right straight into Texas. They ain't nobody in that state knows you until you get to east Texas. Once you're that close to Louisiana, it'll be easy. . . . Besides, it's me these boys really want. They'll come after me . . ."

"How'll they know it's you that rode west?" Blair asked reasonably.

"Hell, that Torrey, he knows every horse we got and who's riding it," Bright said and wondered if Blair was stupid enough to fall for his being set up as the snipe bag holder.

He was. Nodding, Blair said, "I'll tell the boys. You got some money I can give them?"

Bright reached into his saddlebags and dug out a roll of greenbacks and counted out two hundred dollars for the two men who were traveling by stage and two hundred dollars for the men who would eventually take the train. Handing Blair another two hundred dollars, he said, "That should get you all home, but if you get in a bind, you wire the ranch. Able Friday will see that you get some more."

When the men rode out, Bright still sat his horse on top of the hill. When the two men who had been delegated to ride the stage appeared at the livery below, Bright watched them enter the building and then turned his horse's head and rode down to their camp, stepped off the animal, gathered up the bundle of grub his men had set aside for him, stuffed it into a saddlebag, and remounted. Turning south he gigged the animal and headed for Las Cruces where he had a friend. There he would change horses, turning his own mount out with others on the open range and ride east along the New Mexico-Texas line and cross into Texas at Hobbs, New Mexico. They'll have a hell of a time following everybody, he thought, knowing it would be the luck of the draw as to who went after him. I hope it's that bastard, Carroll Rose, he thought, deciding if the gunman came his way, he would bushwhack him and laugh while the long-haired grinning killer kicked out his life.

*   *   *

Vent was eating an early breakfast when he looked up and saw the two riders pass. Casually glancing at the brands, he suddenly froze with spoon halfway to mouth and narrowed his eyes, for riding boldly down the street were two Circle-A gunman. Lowering the spoon, he rose, dropped a coin on the table and left his half-finished meal and went out the back door, walked along the alley until he arrived behind the livery.

From inside, the soft mutter of voices came to him, then he stepped through the door and stopped in the aisle and hands hanging straight down, waited for one of the men to notice him. Looking up, the liveryman saw him and asked, "Can I help you?" and one of the Circle-A punchers raised his head, saw Vent, and stepped away from his horse to clear his gunhand. The second man, his head bent while he uncinched his saddle, continued to undo the latigo until his friend said quietly, "Mert," and then he turned and stared at Vent and eyes wide, moved further away from his horse in an obvious attempt to put Vent in a crossfire.

The liveryman, knowing trouble when he saw it, suddenly turned and without a word, walked into his small sleeping quarters and closed the door.

Now both the Bright men had their hands on their guns and still Vent had not moved. "End of the line, boys," he said and waited.

"Damn you to hell!" one of them suddenly screamed and dove for his gun, catching his partner flat-footed and gaining Vent a good second. Drawing swiftly, he shot the first man in the stomach, then swiveled and planted a slug in the second man's chest, knocking him against a stall, where he managed to get a hand fastened to a pole and keep himself up.

"You damned peckerwood," he groaned and tried to

lift the gun and Vent, showing no compassion, shot him again, knocking him down. Rolling on his back, he began to crawl toward the door and Vent let him go, turning in time to catch the first man with gun coming into alignment, his face contorted with the agony of the effort. Vent, his lips peeled back in a fighting snarl, deliberately triggered two slugs into the man's chest and watched clinically as he went down on his back, rolled over and, toes digging into the dirt, lay gasping for breath. Then he died and Vent looked at the second man and saw he had made the doorway. He lay there, one hand outthrust, the other grasping the butt of his six. He, too, was dead.

Walking to the kicking, squealing horses, Vent spoke soothingly to them and got them quieted. When the liveryman finally stuck his head out the door of his room, the ponies were standing trembling, their eyes walled in fright. Vent glanced at him, then calmly punched the empties from his .44 and reloaded it just as Rand Carpenter and Gil Monroe burst through the door, guns fisted.

Seeing Vent, they both stopped and Carpenter went and checked the bodies and looked up at Monroe and said, "Both corked off."

At that moment Carroll Rose, closely followed by his father, slid through the back door. Both had guns in their hands. Seeing Vent standing quietly against a stall, they reholstered the weapons and Carroll catfooted along the aisle, had his look at the dead men, and said mildly, "Looks like somebody else will be riding these old boys' saddles."

Carpenter stood up, looked at Vent and asked, "Canefield Bright's boys?"

"Yeah," Vent replied. "They rode through town and in here. Probably saw Cap Stalls and his boys leave and didn't know we were still around."

"Their mistake," Monroe said and led the way to the street.

Looking around, Carpenter spotted a dark-clad man in the sizable crowd and called, "Hey, Mr. Peevy. Got a couple of customers in here need tending to," and as the undertaker walked past him, he added, "You should give Mr. Torrey a cut. Everytime he comes to town, you get fresh business."

The undertaker, a singularly somber man lacking any semblance of a sense of humor, glanced absentmindedly at Carpenter, then asked, "He didn't shoot them in the head, did he? I hate it when they're shot in the damn head. Makes a hell of a mess."

Carpenter stared at him, then observed, "Why Mr. Peevy, I didn't know that bothered you. I promise the next time I croak some poor devil, I'll make sure and shoot him in the belly. How's that?"

Peevy grunted and passed inside.

While the Shakespeare undertaker went about his grisly business, Cap Stalls and his men managed to pick up the trail of the two men riding south. One of Stalls' men, a better than average tracker, recognized a hoof print by a slightly crooked shoe and now they were pushing their horses toward Silver City. They caught up with the two men just before dark and when Stalls spotted the riders, he sent four Barbed-T men in a swing around them and led the rest up from behind overtaking them near a small creek. One of the men looked around and then said something to his partner and they gigged their horses into a fast trot, but pulled in when the four Barbed-T riders suddenly rode up out of a wash and cut them off. Sitting his horse in the middle of the trail, Stalls called, "You boys drop your hardware and shuck them rifles. This is the end of the road for you."

"Who you looking for?" one of the men called.

"You," Stalls called back.

"What the hell for?" the man asked.

"For murder," Stalls told him and led his men forward.

When the Barbed-T segundo was ten feet from them, he looked at the brands on their horses and said softly, "Circle-A broncs. Drop the guns," and watched as the men unstrapped their weapons and tossed them into the roadside grass. Two Barbed-T riders came alongside and pulled their rifles from the scabbards and dropped them next to the handguns.

"Hands behind your backs," Stalls ordered coldly.

One of the men, his face white, stared at Stalls and asked shakily, "What the hell you fixing to do, mister?"

"Simple, murderer. We're gonna hang you," Stalls told him.

"Now wait a minute," the second man gasped. "We got a right to a trial. That's the law . . ."

"Hands behind your backs," Stalls said relentlessly.

Riding behind them, two Barbed-T riders used short pigging strings to bind up their victim's arms, then they were led to a big oak tree near the creek and while their horses were held, another Barbed-T man tossed two lariats over a limb and dropped the loops around each man's neck and pulled them tight.

Suddenly one of the men began to cry, shrilling, "Oh my God, men, don't do this. Oh God, my wife and children . . . My poor wife . . ."

Stalls' face looked as if it were carved from stone as he said, "You boys killed Elam Jordan and a lot of good Barbed-T men. You murdered the sheriff and the marshal of Pioche; men who were just doing their jobs. They's a price to pay for such doings, mister, and now's the time for the debt to be called in."

"You don't even know our names," the second man said plaintively.

"Your names are murder," Stalls replied and nodding at his men, moved his horse backward as the doomed punchers' horses were led from beneath them. As the ropes pulled tight, both men struggled frantically to keep their knee grips on their horses, but then they fell away and hung jerking and twitching as their life was choked from them. Staring up into the contorted faces, Stalls said softly, "This here's for you, Whitey, and for you, Elam," and then the first man's body went limp. The second rider took longer to die, but finally, after almost five minutes, he too hung limp and dead, a trickle of blood dripping from the corner of his mouth onto his shirt front.

"Let's ride," Stalls said and turned his horse and headed back toward Shakespeare.

Vent sat looking down at the tangle of tracks leading in several directions from the area of the burned out campfire and knew his quarry had split up on him. Dismounting, he walked around the campfire twice, then moved on to where the Circle-A horses had been staked out. Here the tracks of two horses going toward Shakespeare were plain to see.

Turning to Denton Rose, he said, "Reckon the two boys I put down at the livery was riding them ponies."

"Looks that way," Denton agreed, then Carroll called and Vent and his father walked to where the Texan was standing looking at the churned-up ground. Pointing to two sets of tracks, Vent said, "Two riders went south," then he put his boot toe on another set of tracks and observed, "A single rider going southeast."

Carroll walked east for a hundred feet and turned and called, "A man rode this way," and Vent and Denton went and looked.

Squatting, Vent stared at the track for a long time, then said, "Light man riding this horse . . . probably Crimp Brair."

"How you figure that?" Carroll asked.

"Whoever was riding that single horse southeast was a heavyweight. All four of those Circle-A punchers, including Blair, are lightweights. Bright, he must weigh over two hundred pounds."

"So how we gonna do this?" Denton asked.

Vent stood up and thought a moment, then said, "By all the tracks going south, I'd bet Cap Stalls and his boys trailed those two. If he did, they're either dead or on their way to jail. Since nobody trailed the other two, I reckon we best split up and you and Carroll see if you can run down one of them and I'll take the other."

"Flip a coin?" Carroll asked, digging out a silver cartwheel.

Vent nodded and when the young gunman tossed the coin in the air, said quietly, "Heads," and watched it land in the dust, heads up.

Carroll grinned. "Which one?"

"I'll follow the one going southeast," he smiled.

Walking to his horse, he mounted, waved, and rode south as Carroll and Denton stepped into their saddles and lined out dead east.

Crimp Blair was no fool. He had survived ten years of rambling through the various high-rolling mining towns, where he peddled his gun skills to the highest bidder. Now, as he rode east, he knew he was the wild card in this game and that Canefield Bright was hoping the hunters would trail him and leave Bright to ride free and clear back to Louisiana.

He had no intention of riding into any of the towns in

New Mexico unless he absolutely had to have supplies. So he swung northeast and four days of hard riding put him near Tularosa, where he camped in a dry wash for the night and then moved on the next day, reaching the small town at noon. Riding boldly down its main street, he reined in at the telegraph office and sent a wire to Able Friday at the Circle-T, then led his horse across the street and tied it in front of a mercantile store, entered and came out ten minutes later with an armful of grub, which he hastily shoved into his saddlebags, a sense of forboding warning him not to linger here too long. Looking the street over, he saw nothing untoward, yet he still retained the feeling he was being watched and that whoever was watching was not a friend.

Riding north along the main street he suddenly cut down an alley leading east, then doubled back south and walked his horse to the edge of town, where he sat looking back. He was in time to catch a glimpse of a man hurrying from the marshal's office toward a livery stable and figured Stalls or Leatherhand had wired ahead in an attempt to alert peace officers along the route he was expected to follow.

Cursing, he wheeled his horse and rode south for five miles, then angled east again, pushing his horse harder than he liked, but knowing he had to clear the area, with its scattered ranches and too many chance riders.

Once, when he hit a low hill, he rode to its top and over the other side, then dismounting, crept to a big rock, crouched and watched his back trail. Ten minutes and he saw the horseman. The man was riding with head bent and Blair knew he was being trailed. As he turned to move on, the sun suddenly struck fire from something on the man's chest and he thought, a damn badge toter, and went and mounted and rode down the opposite side of the hill, hit the trail east again and put spurs to his horse. He let the big animal lope for another five miles, then swung him into a small grove of trees backed against a huge pile of boulders, dismounted, pulled his Winchester from its scabbard and found a niche between two rocks that afforded good cover, yet gave him a clear view of the trail.

Half an hour crept by and then he saw his quarry. The man was riding a big gray and was tracking him and Blair thought, now there's a damn fool, and lifted the rifle, centered it on the man's chest and slowly took up the slack.

The rifle jumped in his hands and the lawman suddenly spun in his saddle, slid off the right side of his horse and hit the ground with gun in hand, wildly searching for a target. Blair did not give him one, but instead pounded a second bullet into the man's body and watched him slowly lower his head on his crossed arms and let his pistol slip from dying fingers. Mounting, he rode to where the man lay, stepped off his horse and went and rolled him over, noted the blank, half-closed eyes and let him fall back on his face. Mounting again, he rode to where the gray stood, ears pointing toward its fallen master, eyes wide and questing, and picked up the reins and rode on.

Half an hour later, he came up over a small rise in the trail, found himself staring at five Apaches and suddenly realized he must have entered the Mescalero reservation. Pulling in he raised a hand and then asked, "Any of you speak the white man's tongue?"

A young brave gigged his horse forward and unsmilingly said, "I speak."

Blair nodded. "You see this horse I'm riding? How'd you like to own him?"

"Where you steal?" the Indian asked.

"He ain't stolen," Blair said. "Some men are trailing me. I want to fool them . . ."

The Indian looked around at his friends and spoke rapidly in Apache and they nodded wisely and the boy turned back and asked, "What we have to do to get horse?"

"Nothing much," Blair smiled. "I'll change saddles with the gray and give you the horse. One of you ride him north and turn him out with other horses. The others give me until the sun rides down the sky this far," and he held his hands a foot apart, "and then follow in my tracks for one day."

The Indian grinned. "You pretty smart white man," he said.

Blair grinned back. "I learned that from an Indian," he said. "You'll do it?"

Pointing to the rifle in the lawman's scabbard, the young brave asked, "You leave rifle gun on saddle?"

"Yep. You can have the rifle," Blair assured him.

"It's deal," the Indian said and turned and spoke again to the others and they nodded and, watching them, Blair stepped down, pulled his saddle, led his horse to the gray and unsaddled him, then handed the reins to the Indian and tossed his own saddle back on the gray while two of the Indians saddled the Circle-T horse. Mounting, Blair saluted them and rode east again. When he was three hundred yards away, he looked back and saw one of the Indians break away north riding his horse and grinned.

He arrived at Hobbs with a crick in his neck from looking over his shoulder and riding a horse that had covered far too many miles. Hunting up a livery he turned the footsore gray over to a hostler with orders to take the best care of him, then walked down the narrow main street in search of the Buckeye Saloon. Blair knew this town. He had once ridden for a local rancher here and had spent many nights drinking and gambling in the Buckeye. He walked along the narrow street lined with its Mexican-style adobes, each a miniature walled fort with its heavy wooden door leading into a patio and the house proper.

Turning a corner, he saw the crude dangling sign hanging from chains out over the sidewalk and stopped and had his look and saw nothing that seemed to pose a threat. An old man sat on a wooden bench in front of a barber shop across the street; a girl with a water jug balanced on her head swung into the street from a narrow alley, her long skirt brushing her ankles as she strutted toward him, her hips swinging as only a Mexican girl can swing them, and when she passed, smiled at him. He touched his hat and smiled back. Three horses were tied to a tooth-gnawed hitch rack in front of the saloon. A man stepped from an office down street and the sun, just slipping behind the distant western hills, reflected off the badge he wore and Blair thought, town marshal, and walked on, knowing that if the man challenged him, he would turn and drop him, but the marshal merely glanced his way and then walked south toward a cafe and disappeared inside.

Pushing through the saloon door, Blair stopped just inside to give his eyes time to adjust to the dim light and saw the five men standing along the bar and grinned. Tuck Willowby looked up, took in Blair standing there and turned and said softly, "Looks like you made it," and Blair only nodded and came and leaned against the plank.

"What'll it be, mister?" the bartender asked.

Blair did not look at him. "Whiskey," he intoned and let his eyes travel along the line of Circle-T riders. "See you got my telegram," he said.

Willowby smiled, said, "Got her," and jerking a thumb over his shoulder, asked, "These boys all right?"

"Brian Cade, Doodles Smith, Brook Hanson, Mike Paddock . . . Howdy, boys," and each man nodded as he was named and went back to his drink.

Looking at Willowby, Blair said, "Well, you got the best."

"What's the play?" Willowby, a man known widely in Louisiana and Arkansas as a fast man with a gun, asked, watching Blair's eyes.

"Got me some fellers on my back trail," Blair said. "Got a look at them two days ago. Carroll Rose and his daddy, Denton Rose."

Willowby whistled softly. "Man, when you get someone after you, you choose top drawer . . ."

"I didn't do the choosing," Blair said. "You can hang that brand on Canefield. He gave the orders."

"Where the hell did he get to?"

"Headed west . . . so he said," Blair answered and tilted his drink and tossed it off and set the glass back on the bar. Holding up the bottle the bartender raised his eyebrows and Willowby nodded. Filling Blair's glass, the apron accepted Willowby's coin and walked down the plank, filling the rest of the Circle-T riders' glasses.

"Got some tough news," Willowby said.

Blair looked at him and waited, knowing deep inside that the others had been taken.

"When you fellers split up the Barbed-T followed Abbott and Brown. Caught them south of Shakespeare. They hanged them . . ."

"Jesus!" Blair said and then asked, "The others?"

"Leatherhand killed them in the livery at Shakespeare. The marshal out there wired us with the details. Said Dimmick and Dutchy never even got off a shot. They tried, but Torrey was just too good to beat."

"And now he must be after Canefield," Blair guessed.

"If Carroll Rose is following you, then it stands to reason that Torrey will be on Canefield's trail," Willowby agreed.

"So where does that leave the Barbed-T?"

"Don't know," Willowby shook his head. "They could be after you or following Canefield."

"I've run as far as I'm going to," Blair said grimly. "We're going to set up a little welcoming party for the Roses."

"They got a tough marshal here," Willowby warned.

"If he gets in the way, we'll put him down too," Blair said coldly.

"I reckon it's your fandango," Willowby grunted. "We'll dance along with you," and he tossed off his drink and led the way to the street.

Marshal Bent Turner had been a lawman most of his life, having first pinned on the badge when he was sixteen years old, and still mourning the loss of both parents and his sister in an Indian raid on the Kansas plains. He worked as marshal of Iola, Kansas for two years, then married a local man's daughter and the two of them traveled into Oklahoma where Turner took a badge for Judge Parker, working a year under Heck Thomas. When the job at Hobbs came up, he decided to accept it. His wife had quietly watched as more than thirty Parker deputies died violently trying to clean out the no man's land of west Oklahoma. She had wearied of the clang and clatter of Parker's infamous hanging gibbet upon which he boasted he could string up twelve men at once if need be. She had watched the dark figure of Parker's hangman, George Maledon, stride the streets, often with his fine Kentucky hemp ropes, their ghastly nooses dangling over his narrow shoulders, and knew she would not stay in that place.

Turner, who loved her furiously, finally agreed to leave and then the Hobbs position came along and he grabbed at it.

Sitting over his steak and eggs, he watched his wife moving from stove to table and suddenly knew just how lucky he was.

"They's a hardcase crew down at the Buckeye," he said.

Turning, she looked at him and asked, "Know them?"

"Recognized two of them; Tuck Willowby and Doddles Smith. Third feller rode in this evening and joined them. Could be nothing or they may be up to some kinda mischief."

Watching him chew his steak methodically, she suddenly said, "Bent, why don't we buy the Summers place and leave lawing to other folks?"

He smiled at her and then returned to his meal, for this had been an ongoing discussion between them for a long time. Mary wanted him to get out of law work and try something else. It was all he knew and somehow he couldn't seem to make her understand that. Now, with the Summers ranch up for sale at a good price, she saw an opportunity and had begun pushing at him over a month ago. Thinking about it as he poured his second cup of coffee, he asked himself, why the hell not? He'd been a lawman far too long now. Turner was aware of the odds. He knew that sooner or later he'd make that mistake that every lawman made. If he was lucky, he'd live to tell about it. If he wasn't, Mary would be alone. He did not want her to be alone and he damned sure didn't plan on getting killed, but he was also aware of the chances the job imposed on him. Not liking his thoughts he rose and wiped off his mouth and mustache, dropped the napkin on the table, and went to her and kissed her soundly.

"I'll be home early," he promised. "Want to kinda keep an eye on these strangers. Figure out what they're doing in Hobbs. After I make the midnight check, I'll come home," and putting on his hat he walked to the door and opened it and looked back at her and winked.

"You be careful, Bent Turner, you hear?" she warned.

"Yes ma'am," he answered and went out and quietly closed the door. Once clear of his home he reverted back to the needs of his job and sometimes this made him wonder. How can a feller walk through a door and suddenly discover total peace and security and then come back out that door and find a hostile world waiting for him and become a part of it, he wondered.

Walking up the street, he turned into the barber shop and nodding at Milt Barron, who was just cleaning up preparatory to going home, grinned and observed, "Looks like we got some hardcases hit town?"

Turner nodded. "Looks that way. You recognize any of them?"

Barron, who had barbered in a dozen wild and woolly mining towns, nodded and suddenly serious, said, "One of them fellers is Crimp Blair."

Jerking his head up, Turner stared at him. "The hell you say? Which one?"

"The slim gent with the chino chaps and the gray hat. . . . He rode in this evening . . ."

"I saw him," Turner nodded.

"That's a tough bunch, Bent. Best be damn careful."

"I'll do that," Turner promised and went out and crossed to the Buckeye and went in, leaned on the bar near the door and when the apron came down, ordered beer.

The bartender, who liked the marshal, as did most of the townspeople, brought his beer, said, "First one's on the house," knowing Turner never drank more than one, and leaned his elbows on the mahogany, observing, "We had us some high-toned pistol fighters in here, Bent."

"So I understand. Didn't happen to hear them talking, did you?"

"Yep, as a matter of fact I did. Funny how folks seem to forget the bartender and get loose-mouthed."

Turner smiled. "Say anything that made sense?"

"Said they was waiting for Carroll Rose," the bartender said softly.

"Hey, Johnny," a customer called from down the bar. The bartender went and waited on him, collected his money, and came back to lean on the plank again.

Thinking about it, Turner wondered what the hell was going on. Then the bartender said, "They're gonna take Rose out . . . gonna set up a gun trap for him . . ."

"Well, at least Rose ain't with them," Turner smiled and then he touched the big bartender's arm and added softly, "Johnny, thanks. I owe you one," and before the man could answer, went out the back door and walked quietly along the street until he reached a corner. Turning back east toward the main street he hugged the wall concealing Jesus Martinez' house until he reached the main street. Stepping around the corner, he looked south down the slightly inclined paving blocks and saw only an empty street. Now where the hell did those fellers get to, he asked himself and decided they were probably holed up at the livery. Walking boldly out onto the sidewalk, he lifted the tiedown from his gun hammer and strode north until he reached the stables.

The hostler, an ancient Negro everybody called Shoe, stood in the entranceway chewing on a straw and when he saw Turner, he walled his eyes, rolled them toward the sky, and then looked blank. Without hesitation, Turner passed by, nodded at Shoe, and said softly, "How you, Shoe?" and then he was beyond the structure and had his answer. Circling east, he moved through the narrow streets and alleys like a prowling cat, for he knew every inch of this town and could walk it on the darkest night. He knew where the trash piles were; where the outdoor privys stood and the location of the backyard horse corrals and private stables. Most of the houses had high adobe walls completely surrounding them, a leftover from the days when the Mescalero Apaches roamed this land raiding ranches and towns and killing, raping, burning, and carrying off captives.

When he reached the south end of town, he walked back north again until he reached his office, then sat down in an ancient chair, tilted it back against the wall and sat watching the street. Half an hour crawled by and the town seemed normal. Old Lady Baines, who Turner figured had to be at least ninety-five years old, came along the sidewalk, smiled vaguely in his direction, said, "Hello, Cadwell," and moved on. Cadwell had been the marshal in Hobbs more than ten years ago.

The black hostler from the livery entered the Buckeye for his nightly beer. A pig came along the street, pausing here and there to root in the gutter. When he sensed Turner sitting there, he squealed and ran down an alley. Bob Allen closed and locked the door of the mercantile he ran and trudged north, saying, " 'Night, marshal," as he passed by.

"Evening, Bob," Turner replied, then rose and went inside, unlocked the gun cabinet and brought forth a ten-gauge, double-barreled, sawed-off shotgun of the kind carried by Wells Fargo agents and guards. Breaking it, he selected two shells from a box marked DOUBLE OUGHT and filled the gaping breach, locked the weapon shut, and went back and resumed his former position, the deadly scattergun lying across his lap. He was still sitting there when two men rode in from the south. Hearing the clatter of hooves on the cobble stones, Turner turned and looked down street and saw the dark shape of two horses and riders, but couldn't make them out in the almost full dark. While he watched, they came on carefully, their heads turning as they checked each alley and doorway. When they reached the marshal's office, one of them pulled rein and said softly, "You the marshal?"

"I am," Turner answered, letting the barrel of the shotgun swivel just far enough to cover them.

"Name's Carroll Rose. This here's my paw, Denton. Looking for some fellers who murdered a marshal and sheriff out in Nevada."

"Put a name to them," Turner ordered.

"Man we're after's called Crimp Blair," Carroll said. "Fancies himself a shootist."

"I'd say you got more right to that title than Blair does," Turner observed drily.

Rose chuckled softly, then reminded Turner, "You didn't answer my question."

"Your man's got some friends. Met up here with five gents riding hosses carrying Circle-T brands. Tuck Willowby and Doddles Smith are two of them."

"So . . ." Rose said softly.

Turning his horse then, the younger Rose looked at Turner and the marshal could see the shine of his eyes and teeth in the light from a lantern hanging in front of the saddle shop two doors down.

"Where do you stand in this?" he asked.

"I'm the limb of the law here," Turner answered. "Means if something threatens the town, then I take a hand. You got a personal fight with these fellers, that's your business. Kill somebody by accident, that's my business."

"They's a warrant out for Blair for two counts of murder in Nevada and he's also a suspect in the killing of a sheriff east of here. Was he riding a gray horse?''

"He was," Turner said.

"He killed the sheriff of Otero County and stole that horse," Denton said.

Turner had known the Otero County sheriff and considered him a good man. He wondered vaguely how the lawman had managed to get himself killed by a gunsel like Crimp Blair. Turner knew the sheriff was damn good with a gun. Thinking about it, he said softly, "Knew the feller. Good man.''

"Not good enough," Carroll said bleakly, then gigged his horse. "We'll be around. Be careful," he warned.

Turner watched them pass along the street toward the south end of town and wished he could go fishing.

When the Roses rode around a corner at the end of the block, Turner looked back toward the livery and vaguely wondered why he hadn't warned them Blair and his men planned a gun trap. Thinking about it he was suddenly ashamed and decided to rectify the mistake. Rising, he moved south, the shotgun hanging under his arm. Halfway down the block he met the mayor, who stopped, looked at the sawed-off and asked, "You got problems, Bent?''

"Not yet, Mr. Mayor, but if I was you, I'd kinda stay off the streets," Turner warned.

"Need any help?''

"They ain't after me," Turner said. "Two sides out to shoot each other up. Decided to use our town for the battleground.''

"Let 'em kill each other," the mayor counseled and crossed the street, entering his office and closing the door.

Good advice, Turner told himself, then he was at the corner and moving down the narrow cross street. The Roses were nowhere in evidence and he wondered if they had doubled back toward the north end of town. When he reached the next cross street, he looked both ways. Emptiness. Turning on his heel, he started back toward his office, having decided Carroll Rose was old hand enough to smell a gun trap. Any man who had killed as many men as they said he had just naturally grew eyes in the back of his head or got himself killed mighty damn fast, Turner knew.

When he reached his office, he sat down in the chair again. All his instincts warned him to back away from this one, but a stubbornness had hold of him and he could not shake it off. He would wait and play the cards as they were dealt.

Carroll Rose sat his horse and looked at the livery barn and knew the men who waited for them were inside. He did not know how he knew this, but he did not doubt the accuracy of his instincts. Turning to his father, he said softly, "Those old boys are waiting over there, Paw. . . ."

Denton Rose glanced at the livery barn. Nothing moved in its vicinity. Looking along the street they had just come up, he saw a head poking from a window on the far side of the narrow way. It was hastily jerked back and the faint slam of a shutter being closed came to them on the still air. Suddenly, Denton had a terrible premonition that almost sucked away his breath. He sat stone still for a long moment, then said quietly, "Son, let's ride out of this, now."

Carroll glanced at his father and saw the blood draining from his face and asked calmly, "You sick or something?"

"No, son, just got a bad feeling . . ."

Thinking about it, Carroll suddenly turned his horse and led the way back down the narrow street until they reached the edge of town where a scattering of buildings, some of them perched on the edge of the hills and others out in the sagebrush flats, afforded little cover. Riding in under a small grove of trees, Carroll dismounted and tying his horse to a limb, loosened the cinch as his father took care of his mount.

"Sorry about that back there, boy," Denton said.

"Have a sudden case of the whips and jingles?" Carroll asked.

"Damned right," Denton admitted. "It just didn't seem right, somehow . . ."

"Hell, Paw, I smelled it too," Carroll said.

"Now what?"

Squatting in the dust, Carroll picked up a stick and drew a line on the ground, then raising his head, said, "Paw, this ain't your kinda game. It's mine. How about waiting here for me?"

Denton stared at him. "Hell, son, I taught you how to use that gun. I ain't as fast as you and never was, but I ain't no slouch neither."

Looking at him, Carroll knew his father would never remain behind. Standing suddenly, he tossed the stick away, went to his horse and pulled up the cinch and said, "Then let's go and get this over with."

When they entered the town this time, they rode directly up the main street, pulled in before the hotel, and went in and rented rooms. Turning their horses over to a hostler, who stabled them behind the building, they climbed the narrow stairs and each sought his room.

Denton awoke at dawn in a cold sweat and wondered what the hell was ailing him. Holding out his hand he tried to steady it and couldn't and rose and went to his saddlebags. Rummaging around he found a pint of whiskey and gulped down a huge drink. When the fiery liquid hit the bottom of his empty stomach, he sighed and recapped it and sat it on a chest of drawers then, catching sight of himself in the cracked mirror, looked long and hard and said aloud, "Denton, you are an old man," and pulled on his clothes. Sitting on the bed he stripped his .45 and carefully cleaned it, then reassembled the heavy six-shooter, punched fresh loads into it and dropped it into his holster. Strapping on the gunbelt, he stood up and the knock came at the door.

"Paw?" Carroll called and Denton went and opened it and looked at his son and smiled. The boy was wearing black pants, a long, black gambler's coat, a black hat slanted over his eyes, polished boots and polished gunbelt.

"Ready?" he asked.

Denton nodded and they went downstairs and the marshal came through the door and said, "They're gonna set a gun trap for you."

Looking at him, Carroll asked softly, "You knew this last night?"

"I did," Turner admitted. His eyes were red-rimmed and he needed a shave and Carroll guessed he had stayed up all night.

"Mister Marshal, you married?" he asked.

"I am," Turner said.

"Go home. Eat a good breakfast. Shave and grab a couple hours sleep," Carroll counseled.

"And what will you be doing?" Turner asked.

"Springing a trap, marshal, springing a trap . . ."

"My town, my problem," Turner said stubbornly.

Carroll stared at him then said, "I don't take it kindly when other men, even lawmen, try to take a hand in my games. The less I have to worry about, the easier things are. . . . You know that . . ."

"There's six of them," Turner pointed out.

"And there's two of us and that makes it even . . ."

It was then Turner made his decision. "Good luck," he

said and walked out the back door and down to the next cross street south of the hotel and waited, his shotgun under his arm.

"He'll not go home," Denton said.

"I know," Carroll nodded, then led the way to the middle of the street and said, "You watch south, I'll watch the stable," and turned his back.

"Three men just came from the cafe," Denton said softly.

Then five men walked from the livery and Carroll thought, he's hired some local talent and Denton's voice came low and urgent as he said, "They've doubled on us, son. Two more men . . ."

As the ten gunfighters spread out, five on each end of the street, Carroll called out, "Your mistake, Crimp. You die first," and told his father softly, "Ain't no use waitin', Paw. See you in hell," and the wildcat that lived behind his eyes came bounding out, claws up as he drew both guns and fired them simultaneously. His first slug caught Crimp Blair dead in the guts and the man screamed a hurt animal scream and fell heavily onto the cobblestones as the second man in the line was kicked off his feet by a slug from the .44 Russian.

When Carroll drew, Denton's gun came up in his fist and flamed and a man grunted, ran five feet to the left, and collapsed against a hitchrail, blood pouring from his mouth. Denton fired again and then took a bullet through the shoulder that spun him sideways just as Carroll was hit through the body. Screaming like a madman, the younger Rose fired at a man running toward the left side of the street and scored a hit, tripping him onto his face where he lay struggling feebly to rise. Denton shot a man loose from a porch support and saw him collapse into the street, fired again and knocked a man through a shop window, where he hung half in and half out of the building amid the shattered glass.

Blair lifted his gun, then, and fired and Carroll took the round in the chest and shot back, his bullet ripping through the downed gunman's forehead.

Tuck Willowby fired at Carroll and missed and the youthful gunman answered the shot, putting his bullet through Willowby's heart and knocking him into a water trough. Then Carroll was down on one knee, his .45 held in both hands, his empty .44 at his feet. He shot Brian Cade as the gunman ran toward the corner of the alley. The big slug lifted and hurled him bodily against the side of a building. Ricocheting off the hard adobe, he fell backwards and lay twitching in the middle of the sidewalk.

Doodles Smith took careful aim and shot Denton through the right breast and knocked him down. Turning on his side, the elder Rose fired twice. Both slugs struck Smith in the face, killing him instantly. Brook Hanson and Mike Paddock were down and dying as Carroll put a killing shot into one of the hired Hobbs gunnies.

As suddenly as it had started, it was over. Denton lay on his side, a great pool of blood surrounding his body. He was dead. Carroll, still on one knee, slowly sat down, his head hanging. As men came along the street, led by the running Turner, they stared in amazement. The site of the gunfight looked like the inside of a slaughterhouse. There was blood everywhere. A great smear marked the side of an adobe office building. Blood ran in rivulets between the niches in the cobblestones. There was blood on the sidewalk and the bullet-blasted bodies of the dead Circle-A men were splattered with their own gore.

Turner skidded to a stop and stood staring in horror at the human shambles. Then, above the soft awed murmur of the crowd, he heard the distinct sound of a pistol being cocked and triggered over and over again and walked to where Carroll sat, his empty gun in his hand. Even as Turner stared down at him, Carroll eared back the hammer and pulled the trigger.

"Jesus God!" Turner exclaimed and Carroll, hearing his voice, raised his head and his eyes were still overflowing with the unveiled lust to kill.

"It was a hell of a fight," he muttered and fell sideways and rolled onto his back. The empty gun dropped from his hand and then as the stunned townsfolk stared, he dipped his hand beneath his coat and drew a knife and died.

Mary Turner carried the bean pot out to the wagon and carefully stowed it aboard, then turning to her husband, said, "Best keep good care of that. Looks like we may be using it a lot in the future."

Turner grinned and bent and quickly kissed her and said, "Hell, Mary, they ain't nobody on God's earth can make beans like you can."

As he stepped away, she looked up at him and asked softly, "Bent, I've been wondering. Why didn't you take a hand in that fight?"

Walking to the wagon, he leaned his elbows against it and said quietly, "I damned near did, but then I thought of you sitting at home waiting for me and I thought of the odds up there in the street. I couldn't do it . . . and I also knew in that instant I could no longer be a lawman . . ."

"Could you have saved them?" she asked, searching his tough face.

"I doubt it. I think I would have been dead now . . . and that's why I'm quitting. When a lawman reaches the point where he begins to bargain with himself over his own life, he is no longer fit to carry the badge . . ."

"They say there's some very nice country in Oregon," she observed.

Stepping to her then, he put his arms around her and looking down into her eyes, told her, "Anyplace will be fine with you there."

When Bent drove the wagon through town, several businessmen came out into the street and shook his hand and nodded solemnly at Mary. Then the wagon wheels passed over a place in the middle of the cobblestones where the stone had been turned red and Turner looked down and thought, I would have spoiled it for them if I'd taken a hand, and knew he was right, but also knew his wife could never understand how it was with men who lived by the gun.

Chapter Nine

The big man sat his horse as if he had been in the saddle far too many miles. He had ridden into Las Cruces two days ahead of Vent Torrey, hunted up his friend and swapped horses, and rode out on a tough line-backed buckskin with more than its share of bottom. Knowing a man on the run is a fool to linger over his beer, Canefield Bright had one quick drink, bought some grub at a store, and headed south. Now, as he approached the Texas-Mexico line just north of the stage station at Pumpville, he pulled the horse to a stop and sat looking across the mile of open ground toward the huddle of buildings marking the stopover for the Del Rio to El Paso stage.

Seeing nothing that could offer him a threat, he shrugged and rode on, keeping a tight rein on the buckskin and eyeing the buildings carefully.

Half a mile from them he stopped again and had another look and, satisfied, rode boldly into the yard in front of the station, walked his horse to a water trough and sat while the animal sucked up great gulps of water. When the horse had taken his fill, Bright threw his right leg over the saddle horn and dropped off and, hanging his hat on the horn, stepped to the trough and scooped up a double handful of water and dumped it into his long hair, then followed it with a second double handful which he splashed into his face. Shaking his head, he went to the pump and, working the squeaking handle, brought up cold, fresh water from the underground lake that fed it and drank directly from the spout, then continued to pump until he had refilled the trough.

He recovered his hat and clapped it on his head. Walking toward the station, he looked up and a man was leaning against a porch support on the long veranda fronting the yard. He nodded and Bright, ignoring him, went to the hitch rack, tossed the reins around it in a double wrap, loosened the cinch and, leaving the stirrup hooked over the saddle horn, moved up the steps and entered the cool confines of the station.

As he made his way to the bar, he glanced around. Two men sat at a table in the back of the room playing a desultory game of double solitaire, full beer glasses at their elbows. An Indian slept in a chair, his blanket partially covering his face, his hat cocked over his eyes. A woman standing in the entranceway to the kitchen looked boldly at Bright, then turned back inside, glancing quickly over her shoulder as she closed the door. There was no one behind the bar and Bright walked around the plank and checked the bottles, picked out one labeled sour mash whiskey and went hunting for a glass.

One of the men looked up and said mildly, "If I was you, I wouldn't do that."

Bright stopped, stared at him and said coldly, "You ain't me," found a glass and filled it, recorked the bottle and a man came in the back door, stared at Bright and asked, "Just what the hell do you think you're doing, mister?"

"Getting a drink," Bright answered mildly.

"Well, hell, are you so all-fired thirsty you can't wait to be served like other folks?" the man said.

"You the station manager?" Bright asked.

"I am," the man replied. He had a pugnacious jaw, hard blue eyes and long arms that hung down near the butts of twin .44s.

"What's your name?"

The station manager stared at Bright, then said, "Austin Wagner . . . Who the hell are you?"

"A thirsty customer," Bright said and tossed a silver dollar on the bar and went and sat down, carrying the bottle with him.

Wagner walked to the bar, picked up the silver dollar, looked at it carefully and then dropped it into his pocket.

"You got any grub around here?" Bright asked.

"Chili or stew. Both are good . . ."

"Chili," Bright ordered and Wagner hesitated, then went through the door behind the bar and when he came out, he was followed by the woman, who carried a tray with a large bowl of steaming chili on it, surrounded by half a dozen slices of bread. Placing the food in front of Bright, she looked into his eyes, said, "That'll be half a dollar," and collected his money when he dropped it on the table and went away. Bright turned and ignoring Wagner's frown, watched the woman's butt as she moved out of the room.

Dropping his hands below the bar, Wagner said softly, "Mister, I reckon you best eat and then drift on out of here."

Bright looked up and noting the position of Wagner's hands, grinned and fired over the lip of the table. The smashing roar of the big .45 shattered the room's quietness, galvanizing the two card players into action. They hit the floor flat out on their faces as Bright's bullet tore through Wagner's skull, blowing a large piece of it against the backbar mirror and shattering it. Dead on his feet, the station master was hurled into the rack of bottles and falling, carried them down with him in a cascade of broken glass and sour-smelling whiskey.

The kitchen door whipped back on its hinges and the woman was standing there, rifle in hand. Seeing the carnage behind the bar, she lifted the weapon and aligned it on Bright and he dropped sideways as she fired and shot her through the chest. As the bullet ripped into her vitals, she screamed and fell on top of her husband's body and drew her legs up and thrashed briefly and died.

The Indian sat very still, his hat on the floor, his face unreadable.

Staring at the two men lying in the sawdust, Bright suddenly rose and his eyes filled with madness, walked over. One of the card players looked up and cried, "Oh my God, I ain't armed!" and Bright shot him in the face, then swiveled the .45 and shot the other man as he rose to his feet and started to run for the back door. The bullet drove him into the wall, where he clung for a long moment, his voice coming from his open mouth in mewling cries of agony. As he lost his grip and toppled back, Bright ran outside and when he caught a glimpse of the man he had met on the porch riding at a run to the north, leaped down the steps, jerked his rifle from its scabbard, leveled it across the saddle, and fired. For a long moment he thought he had missed, then the rider suddenly loosed his hold on the saddle and dropped into the sagebrush, turned a complete somersault and tumbled against a rock, where he lay unmoving.

Deliberately then, Bright took careful aim and planted a

second .30.30 slug in the downed man, saw the body jerk and was satisfied the rider was dead.

Walking back inside, he sat down and looking around at the shambles of the station, said softly, "Man should never leave a witness behind," and finished his meal. The Indian had disappeared.

Meal finished, the murderer went out and checked the barn and tack room, but found no one. Satisfied, he cinched up the buckskin and mounting, rode southeast.

That night he camped on the Rio Grande three miles from Langtry, Texas.

Vent rode up out of the shallow draw and pulled in the Appaloosa. A scatter of buildings squatted on the desert half a mile from where he sat and he thought, Pumpville Stage Station, and touched the Appy lightly with his spurs and rode slowly toward the sprawling layout. As he came around the corner of the station, a man looked up from where he was standing near a dust-covered Overland stage and dropped his hand to his gun. Vent spoke softly to the big spotted horse and when the animal halted, he looked at the man and said softly, "I wouldn't if I was you."

Vent's hands lay laxly over the saddle horn and he appeared completely at ease. The man with his hand on his gun was not fooled. He had seen his share of bad ones and now, looking at this tall, quiet-eyed man riding the big Appaloosa, he decided the better part of valor was to find something else to do with his hands so he dug out his tobacco instead. As he carefully rolled a smoke, a second man came from the station. When he saw Vent sitting his horse quietly near the corner of the building, he stopped and dropped a hand to one of the twin .45s he wore, his eyes coldly alert.

"Who the hell are you?" he snapped.

Vent took in the badge, the low-hung guns and the man's alertness and glanced again at the stage. No horses were near the conveyance and he thought, trouble here, and looking again at the lawman, asked, "Trouble, sheriff?"

"Yeah, and maybe you had something to do with it," the sheriff said, his slow Texas drawl deceptively misleading. Vent knew the man was cocked and ready. Smiling, he said, "Just rode in here, Mister Sheriff. Name's Vent Torrey. Looking for feed and water for my horse."

"You want me to knock him outa that saddle?" a voice called from the porch and Vent calmly looked at the man, who stood braced against the wall, a 30.30 rifle leveled at the Missourian's chest.

"Mister, if you don't take that rifle off me, I'm going to blow you loose from it," he said and winter winds were in his voice.

"The hell you say?" the man with the rifle marveled.

"Put it down, Slyde," the sheriff ordered and the man lowered the rifle.

Ignoring them, Vent rode to the water trough, allowed the Appaloosa to drink his fill, then stepped down and dropping the horse's reins, moved out in the middle of the yard and leveled a gun bore look at the sheriff and said quietly, "I asked you a question, lawman."

"You say your name's Torrey?" the sheriff asked.

At that moment a tall man wearing a bowler hat and carrying a gold topped cane came from the building and upon seeing Vent, grinned and, noting the wire-taut sheriff and his men, said mildly, "Gents, meet Leatherhand."

" 'Lo Bat," Vent nodded. "How you?"

"Pretty fair, Vent. This here's some outa your stamping grounds, ain't it?"

The sheriff came over and stuck out his hand and said, "Why didn't you say you was. Leatherhand? Hell, I never heard your given name . . . I'm Hump Bowling, Terrell County Sheriff.''

Shaking his hand, Vent smiled and pointed out, ''You fellers seemed just a bit tense here. . . . What happened?''

Nodding toward the station, Bowling said, ''Come along,'' and led the way inside. Bat Masterson followed them in and then Vent stopped short as the others placed handkerchiefs over their faces and stared at the dead bodies. Seeing the sprawled shape of a woman, he shook his head, looked at the sheriff and asked, ''How long they been dead?''

''About two to three days, but in this heat . . .''

''We found another one,'' one of the deputies who had been outside said from the doorway. It was obvious he did not want to come inside.

Looking at Masterson the sheriff shrugged and led the way outside, where the deputy pointed. The one called Slyde was bent over something lying three hundred feet from the station. Even from where Vent stood, he could see the man held a red bandana over his mouth and nose.

They walked out and Bowling looked down and shook his head. ''It's young Caldwell. Damn!''

A great hole a man could slide a silver dollar in showed through the cloth-ripped back of the dead cowboy's shirt. Looking at it, Vent said sourly, ''Plugged in the back.''

''Come along, Slyde,'' the sheriff ordered. ''I want you and Lee to get a couple of shovels and put these fellers underground,'' and, walking around to the south side of the station where six people, including two women, sat on benches beneath half a dozen shade trees, he said, ''I need a couple of volunteers to help dig graves.''

A lean cowboy, his face burned dark mahogany by the blistering heat of the south Texas sun, rose and said, ''I'm one,'' and went around the building.

A second man, this one obviously a farmer, got up and, shaking his head, said, "God knows, I've had my share of digging graves in this damn country," and followed the cowboy.

"The rest of you will have to wait until we get things sorted out here," Bowling counseled. "Your driver's over to the barn getting a team ready and as soon as he gets 'em hooked up, you can move on. He'll fix up some kinda grub you can take along."

A young woman, her face showing the ravages of hard frontier life, handed a baby to an older woman and stood up, took a deep breath, and said, "I can fix something so we can eat out here."

Bowling said softly, "Thanks ma'am, but that ain't no place in there for a woman."

"I've seen worse, sheriff," she countered. "I came into this country when the Sioux were raiding. They slaughtered my uncle, my father, and my little nephew. Nothing could be worse than that."

Nodding, the sheriff turned and walked back around to the front of the building and as she started up the steps, Vent removed his neckerchief and handed it to her. "Here, ma'am, you'll need this."

"Thank you," she said and placing the cloth to her nose, followed the sheriff inside.

A man came from the barn leading a six-up team and Vent went and took two of them and helped the driver hook them up. When the last trace was snapped in place, the driver climbed to the high seat and, shoving the brake tight, hooked the reins around the handle and climbed down. The horses, better trained than most stage horses, stood with heads lowered, waiting.

Walking over to the water trough, Vent removed his hat and doused his head and face and replaced his hat.

"Going anywhere in particular, Vent, or just drifting?" Masterson asked. He had come up quietly while Vent was washing and now he leaned on his cane, his bowler hat tilted over one eye, his pearl-handled .45 jutting from a cross draw holster worn high on the left hip.

"After a feller," Vent said.

Masterson looked at him sharply. "Would your man do this?"

"He did it," Vent said.

"How do you know that?"

"Tracks," Vent explained. "He's riding a buckskin. Old pony left hair on bushes all the way from Las Cruces to here. Must be shedding its winter coat. Tracks match too."

"You trailed him in here?"

Vent nodded. "He was the only horseman that came and went," and he gestured at the ground near the trough and said, "See that off right hoof? They's a bent nail in it."

Masterson walked over and squatted down and had his look, then followed the tracks for several hundred feet east. Turning back he walked to the northwest of the station and began quartering south, finally stopping and gazing west, then walking that way. Once again he moved along the trail, eyes down reading the buckskin's sign. Finally satisfied he turned and came back to the station just as the sheriff walked from the building.

Glancing at Masterson, he asked, "See anything, Bat?"

Masterson nodded. "Mr. Torrey's following a gent. His is the only tracks in and out of here."

Bowling looked at Vent sharply and then asked, "You mind telling me who you're after and why?"

Vent thought about it. Deciding telling Bowling wouldn't hurt, he squatted in the dust and looking up, said, "Feller's name is Canefield Bright. Killed a sheriff and a city marshal over in Nevada.''

''The hell you say? Canefield Bright? My God, what happened to the rest of the Brights?''

''Mick O'Reilly killed Bobby in a gunfight at Pioche,'' Vent told him. ''The others were downed in a shootout with Carroll Rose.''

''Rose, well maybe that explains what happened in Hobbs, New Mexico a few days ago,'' Masterson said.

Looking at the famous lawman sharply, Vent asked, ''What was that?''

''Carroll Rose and his daddy took on ten men from Bright's outfit. Killed all ten in the damnedest shootout New Mexico ever saw.''

Vent knew what was coming but he had to ask. ''The Roses?''

''They went down too,'' Masterson said bleakly.

Vent looked out across the desert, squinted his eyes against the dancing sun devils and said softly, ''I knew those fellers. Both good men.''

Vent rode out of Pumpville an hour later, after replenishing his water supply and helping himself to some grub, which he packed into his saddlebags. Leaving money for the food with the stage driver, he shook hands with Masterson and nodded at the sheriff, who said, ''I could ride along with you, Mr. Torrey.''

Vent shook his head. ''Like I told you, sheriff, this here's my fight.''

''What if you don't come up on him before he crosses into Louisiana?'' Bowling asked.

''Then I follow him right to his damn doorstep,'' Vent vowed, nodded and rode out.

Now he was half a mile from Langtry, Texas and grinned

sourly when he thought of Judge Roy Bean, the self-proclaimed "only law west of the Pecos."

When he rode up to the Jersey Lilly Saloon, named for the stage actress, Lilly Langtry, as was the town, he found the judge taking the afternoon breezes on the front porch, his spurs hooked over the railing, his hat cocked forward as he lounged in an old rocker.

"Howdy, stranger," the judge said.

Vent nodded, said, "Judge Bean, how you?"

Looking between his boot toes the judge asked, "Do I know you?"

"Name's Vent Torrey from Missouri," Vent smiled.

"Leatherhand," the judge said it as if he was pronouncing sentence.

"About it," Vent agreed.

Lowering his boots to the porch floor, Bean pushed his hat back and observed, "They say you travel mostly west of the Rockies. Long ways from that country . . ."

"Looking for a man," Vent said.

The judge smiled sourly. "Well, at least they ain't looking for you. Who'd the feller kill?"

"Two lawmen and the station manager at Pumpville and his wife and two hired hands. Also shot a young feller in the back who just happened to be stopping by."

"Sounds like you got your work cut out for you," Bean observed.

"Reckon," Vent agreed.

Standing up and stretching, the judge said, "Come along, Mr. Torrey. I'll buy you a drink," and led the way inside where half a dozen men either leaned against the bar or played cards at a table near the back of the room.

Vent joined the judge at the bar and looking up, stared at the life-sized portrait of Lilly Langtry and said, "She's a beautiful lady."

"That she is," the judge agreed and lifted his glass and said, "To the Jersey Lilly," and Vent echoed it and they drank and Vent shook hands and as he turned to leave, Bean told him, "You catch that feller in my jurisdiction, bring him back here, and I'll see he's hanged all proper and legal."

"I'll do that," Vent promised and went out and mounted the Appaloosa, rode to a water trough, and allowed the animal to drink, then stepped down and filled his canteens and remounted and rode east. As he reached the edge of the scatter of buildings that made up Langtry, he glanced north and saw proof of the effectiveness of the judge's sentences; a man swung from a crude scaffold, his body twisting and turning in the warm wind that blew down from northern Texas.

"Pretty final," Vent observed and gigged the Appaloosa and rode on.

Four days later he trotted through Eagle Pass and it was here his quarry broke northeast, heading for Pleasanton. When Vent rode down the dusty main street of the cow town, he knew he must lay over or change horses, as the Appaloosa was beginning to show the strain. Hunting up a livery stable, he turned the tired horse over to a hostler with orders to rub him down, water him slow, grain him, and stall him with a bait of good hay. He gave the man a five dollar gold piece to assure the best treatment and left the man testing the coin between his teeth.

Hunting up a restaurant, Vent went to the back of the room and eased into a chair as a red-headed waitress with more freckles on her face than his horse had spots, came over and smiling, asked, "What'll it be, cowboy?"

"Steak, eggs, potatoes, biscuits, and gravy. Toss in a pot of coffee while you're at it. I'm tired of my own cooking."

"A handsome feller like you sure as hell wouldn't have to do his own cooking around here," the girl smiled and walked away, swinging her backside. Vent grinned. He liked the bluntness of Texas women. With them a man knew exactly where he stood.

While he ate, the city marshal, a dour-looking man with a long face adorned by a walrus mustache, came in and took a table near Vent. When the waitress came, she grinned at him, accepted his order, said, "Cheer up, Milt, it ain't that bad," and, throwing Vent a wink, went back to the kitchen. Vent had heard the lawman order vegetables, a bowl of soup and some crackers, and decided he probably had stomach trouble.

Looking over at Vent he nodded and said sourly, "Damn gut's been giving me hell. Cain't eat a thing . . ."

"Damned shame," Vent agreed as he stuffed large chunks of steak into his mouth and chewed with relish. Watching him the marshal finally said with great disgust, "Dammit, stranger, couldn't you look just a little less happy about that there steak?"

Glancing over at him Vent said, "Sorry as hell, marshal. Should have realized," and cut off another large slice and put it in his mouth and began chewing it very slowly, gazing toward the street with a solemnly happy expression on his face.

Then the waitress brought the marshal's order and he sat and gazed at it as if somebody had dropped a large cow pie on his plate and suddenly pushed it back and looking at the redhead, said, "To hell with it, Sissy. Bring me the same thing that feller's got," and she picked up his food and turned and stopped at Vent's table and said, "He does that every time."

"Cain't say as I blame him," Vent replied. "If a feller has to eat like a rabbit, he's better off in Boot Hill."

The marshal threw Vent a grateful look and observed, "Me, I done thought about swallowing my gun barrel half a dozen times."

"Been to a sawbones?" Vent asked.

The redhead smiled. "Hell no, he ain't been to no sawbones. He's feared of what they'll tell him. Just suffers along with it and we all suffer too 'cause it makes him a mean lawman."

"I ain't no mean lawman," the marshal protested, then added, "but if you don't fetch me my food, Sissy Cortland, I'm gonna get mean and tan your britches."

Looking boldly at Vent she observed, "Now that's the best damn proposition I've had in a month," and went to the kitchen.

Looking at the marshal, Vent noted his face was red. "Damn baggage," the marshal growled. "Younguns just ain't got no respect for their elders nowadays . . ."

Finished with his meal, Vent poured himself a cup of coffee from the pot the waitress had left sitting on a brick at the edge of his table and looking at the marshal, said, "Marshal, I'm looking for a feller. You might be able to help me . . ."

The marshal's eyes grew wary, then, as he asked, "You a lawman?"

"No, just a man who owes some dead fellers a debt. Trying to collect . . ."

"I see. Mind telling me who you are?"

Vent hesitated, then said softly, "Name's Vent Torrey. Some folks call me Leatherhand."

Looking pointedly at the odd glove Vent wore, the marshal said, "Thought maybe that's who you were. I doubt they's a lawman in the west who don't know about that glove. You as fast as they say you are?"

"I reckon I'm fast enough," Vent countered.

The marshal thought about that for a bit, then observed, "Killing Jim Miller put forty or fifty gents in the ground, but then he wasn't too bashful about where he plugged them. I heard you passed his score some time back, the only difference being you shoot from the front."

Smiling bleakly, Vent said quietly, "Don't count 'em."

Looking at him with new respect the marshal nodded. "Don't reckon I would either . . . Who you after?"

"Feller name of Canefield Bright . . ."

Then the waitress brought the marshal's food and as she placed the platters in front of him, his eyes began to gleam, and picking up knife and fork, he carved off a large chunk of steak, thrust it into his mouth and with a blissful expression on his face, slowly masticated it.

"Canefield Bright, huh?" he said around the steak. "The Circle-A Ranch over in Louisiana. More than 250,000 acres of land. Close to 5,000 head of prime beef and enough horses to mount the Seventh Cavalry. That's Canefield Bright."

"If he gets back to Louisiana, he's gonna be the devil's own sidekick to pry loose," Vent said sourly.

"What about his kinfolk? Hell, he's got brothers and a paw; all gun savvy as hell."

"All dead," Vent told him. "Killed by Carroll Rose."

The marshal stared at him. "Carroll Rose . . . Our cross to bear . . ."

Vent shook his head. "Not anymore, he ain't. Killed at Hobbs, New Mexico by a bunch from the Circle-A. Both Roses went down, but they carried ten men with them to row the boat across the river."

"The hell? I knowed old Denton. Hell of a good man. Always thought the boy was addled in the head; sorta kill-crazy."

"He was one of the fastest men I ever met," Vent said.

Looking at the tall Missourian, the marshal asked, "Could you have beat him?"

Vent grinned. "Damned if I know. Maybe . . . Maybe not. Feller never has an answer to that question until he's looking over his gun barrel at the other gent."

"That's a true story," the marshal said, then looking at his food, told Vent, "If you'll wait until I get on the outside of this, we'll kind of drift around town and ask some questions . . . My name's Milt Brown."

Half an hour later they walked into the livery stable and the marshal called the hostler over and asked him, "Keno, you had anybody in here the last week or so riding a lineback buckskin?"

"Sure," the hostler said promptly. "Come along out back," and he led the way through the back door to where several horse corrals held half a dozen horses. Pointing, he said, "Yonder he stands. Feller swapped me for a fresh horse. This one, he's about done in, but I reckon he'll make his feed if I can find somebody that likes linebacks."

"This gent, was he a big man, a two-hundred-pounder?" Vent asked.

"Yep. Hell, lot of folks in this part of Texas knows them Brights. They used to come here and buy cattle. This was one of the boys, Canefield, I think . . ."

"What color horse did you trade him?" the marshal asked.

"Why, that blaze-faced sorrel," the hostler said. "He rode him around town a little. Liked his stride. That horse could reach out further than any old pony I ever had."

Vent handed the hostler another five dollar gold piece and thanked him, then turned to the marshal and invited, "Drink, Mr. Brown?"

So they had a drink at the Tumbleweed Saloon and then Vent hunted up a hotel and, renting a room, fell into bed and slept for twenty-four hours. He awoke fresh and ready to travel, but decided on a bath first. With a month's accumulation of dirt scrubbed away and clean clothes on, his gun cleaned, oiled, and loaded with fresh shells, he felt as if he could ride another thousand miles. And then thinking about it, he suddenly realized that that was just about how far he had chased Canefield Bright.

Returning to the restaurant where he had eaten before, he ordered another meal similar to the last one, smiled and winked at the waitress and received a wink in return, and fell to eating. When he finally pushed back his plate, the redhead came and piling the dishes in a stack preparatory to cleaning up the table, looked Vent directly in the eyes and asked, "How long you staying?"

Meeting her look for a long moment he finally said quietly, "I reckon I'll be around another night."

Taking a deep breath, she said softly, "They's a little white house at the end of First Street. Kinda hidden back in the trees. Drop around if you're a mind to," and walked away.

Thinking about it, he decided, what the hell, and dropping some coins, went back to the hotel, slept some more, waking at full dark. Rising, he went to the water basin, slopped cold water into his face, smoothed back his hair and readjusted the leather glove on his right hand. Looking at himself in the mirror, he grinned an odd grin, put on his hat and left the hotel, walked the short distance to where the cottage sat back among the trees, went to the door and knocking lightly, waited, hat in hand.

The door opened and the redhead was standing there looking at him. "My name's Sissy," she said. "I'm glad you came," and her breasts rose and fell with her breathing.

"I've always liked redheads," he said and went in.

Closing the door behind him, she said, "I'm glad,"

and, taking him by the hand, led him toward the back of
the house.

"What's back here?" he asked.

"The bedroom," she said almost shyly.

"Well, I'll be damned," Vent marveled.

Canefield Bright knew Vent Torrey was still somewhere
behind him. He didn't have to see the tall Missourian to
know that. He could feel it deep in his guts. He had
stopped briefly at Huntsville for grub, but left hurriedly
after seeing the prison there. The cold stone walls gave
him the shivers. Riding by them he couldn't imagine what
it would be like to spend one's life locked up in such a
place. I'd hold court in the street, he thought, and gigged
the sorrel into a trot, quickly leaving the town and its grim
tenant behind.

That night he camped in a low draw near a stream and
built a small fire, cooked a frugal meal and ate quickly,
then sat with his back against a tree drinking coffee.
Nearby the blaze face cropped the rich grass, working out
at the far end of its picket rope. He had heard the news of
what happened at Hobbs and as he sat there, he wondered
how the hell a man got this deep in a thing. It had all
started with Bobby, a useless pup his father had kicked out
a long time ago. If the old man hadn't insisted they ride
west to avenge the kid, he'd be back at the ranch right now
sitting on the front porch smoking and talking to his father
and brothers. Instead, he was the only survivor and he had
a human bloodhound on his trail. He did not delude himself that he could beat Vent Torrey in a gunfight. He was
good, but not that good. He didn't even think he could get
away with bushwhacking him. The man had survived a
long time and they said he was one of the few men in the
west who could beat the Apache at his own creep-and-

crawl game. No, all Canefield Bright could do was keep running and hope he made the Louisiana line ahead of Leatherhand. Thinking about it, he wondered if the famous gunman would have the nerve to follow him into his own stamping grounds and decided he probably did.

Bright knew one thing; when he got back he was going to fire Able Friday. He had wired the foreman asking that men be sent to meet him in Pleasanton. He had received a terse wire in return in which Friday had merely stated, "Can't spare them," and so now he was on his own.

Looking at the fire he had a sudden premonition that he'd never see the Circle-A again and his soul was filled with a great bleakness as he thought of the killings behind him and wondered what in hell had happened to him to push him so far that he even stooped to killing women.

"I reckon there's a time for every man to die," he said aloud and realized he was already accepting a fate he was certain he could not avoid.

The Appaloosa went lame two miles west of Nacogdoches and Vent was forced to dismount and lead the animal into town. He found a cluster of adobe and board and bat shacks set down in the middle of cow country and was grateful the place at least had a livery stable. When he walked into the barnlike structure, he found a man tacking a set of shoes on a big black horse whose eyes were walled and teeth bared.

Glancing up the man growled, "Be with you in just a bit, friend, that is unless this ornery bastard kicks my damn head out into the corral," and as if it could understand him, the stud suddenly fired a hoof past the liveryman's head, coming close enough to knock his hat off and driving a board through the wall.

"Goddamn you, you wall-eyed son-of-a-bitch!" the liveryman shouted and whacked the stud on the neck with his rasp.

Startled by the sudden blow, the animal kicked backwards again, this time with both hind feet. Vent dodged around him and grabbed an ear, clamped his teeth into it and jerked the stud's head down. The animal immediately quit kicking and stood with head cocked, slobbering down the front of Vent's chaps.

"I'll hold him, you shoe him," Vent said.

"Thanks, friend," the liveryman said gratefully and quickly nailed the back shoes on, crimped the nails and seating them, filed down the tips. Dropping the off hoof, he said, "You can turn the mean bastard loose now, and thanks again."

Vent stepped away from the stud as the animal shook his ears and then walled his eyes at Vent. "Never cared much for a stud," Vent said.

Glancing at the Appaloosa the liveryman asked, "What can I do for you?"

"Horse came up lame," Vent replied. "Had to lead him the last couple miles into town."

"Wait until I stall this ornery varmint and I'll have a look," he promised and led the black to a rear stall and, after half a dozen abortive attempts, finally got him inside and tied up. Coming back, he observed, "That there's the meanest damn horse in this part of the country. Don't know why the hell old Jack Shaker rides him, anyway. He's kicked the living hell out of him twice," and he bent and picked up the Appy's leg and felt the tendons.

Going over the lame ankle very carefully, he finally set the hoof down and said, "Nothing serious. Hoss has a strained tendon. Give him a week and he'll be fine as a fiddle again."

"You got a rental horse?" Vent asked.

"Sure have, several. How long you want him for?"

"If you can tell me how many days ride it is to the Louisiana line, I can tell you how long I need him for," Vent said.

"About two days to the Sabine River, I'd guess."

"Figure six days," Vent said.

"Cost you twenty, but I'll take three off that 'cause of you being neighborly and helping me with that stud. If anything happens to the horse you pay for him and if you ain't back in thirty days, I keep the Appy. Agreed?"

Vent shook hands with him and asked, "You want the money now?"

"When you get back'll be fine . . . What's you're name?"

"Name's Vent Torrey," Vent said and watched his face. The liveryman looked at him for a long time, then grunted. "You'll get back. Have a good trip," and went for the horse.

When Vent left Nacogdoches, he was up on a long-legged gray whose strides ate up the miles as if getting to the other end of the ride was more important to him than eating. That night he passed through the border town of Sexton at ten o'clock and was a mile from the river when daylight came in the form of a blazing sun tilting over the edge of the world, sending its slanting rays into his eyes. Tilting his hat forward, he rode on, glancing occasionally at the ground where the sorrel's tracks showed plainly in soil made damp by a recent rain.

The trail here was narrow and crowded on both sides by timber and a tangle of brush that made for a perfect ambush if Bright decided to try it. Vent didn't think the man would attempt it this close to the Sabine but still he rode with caution.

When the shot came, he was half expecting it in spite of

thinking the man from Louisiana wouldn't stop to lay a gun trap this close to home. The slug, fired from a Winchester, drilled the gray square between the eyes and Vent, even as he threw himself free of the falling animal, knew the horse had saved his life, for it had lifted its head back in an attempt to shake off a swarm of swamp flies at the same instant the shot came, thus catching the bullet meant for him.

Cursing savagely, he hit the ground rolling as the hidden rifleman pounded three more rapid shots at him. One of them dug a piece of leather from his boot heel, hit the rowel of his spur, and set it spinning wildly. Vent palmed up his gun and fired twice and heard thrashing in the brush, then silence. Sliding further back away from the trail, he found himself on a parallel trail and rising, ran full tilt along it until he was past where the shots had come from, then he broke back to the old trail again and heard hoof beats and looked up in time to see a horse whirl around a bend to the east of him and fired. It was a clean miss, but Bright turned in the saddle, his lips peeled back in triumph, and was swept from his saddle when the free-running animal suddenly passed under a limb.

The Louisianian hit the ground with a grunt and although obviously shaken by the fall, managed to roll from the trail into the brush. Vent ducked down just as Bright fired and heard the snap of the slugs as they passed his head. They were uncomfortably close. Scooting deeper into the tangle, he waited for Bright's next attempt. Half an hour went by and nothing moved out there. Deciding to hell with it, Vent rose and ducked across the trail, expecting a hail of lead, but no shots came. Running through the trees, he passed the place where Bright had gone to ground. He wasn't there any longer. Vent skidded to a stop, looked at the tracks and saw the man had moved due south. His boot heels had left deep gouges in the leafy mold and were easy to follow.

Vent smelled the river before he reached it and wondered if Bright had managed to catch up his horse. Then he saw light ahead and suddenly he was standing at the edge of an open field that reached to the banks of the Sabine. Nothing moved out there and, with a sinking feeling, Vent knew the man had caught his horse and was probably even now racing north or south.

Cursing under his breath, he was about to step into the open when a bullet ripped a large chunk of bark from the tree where he was crouched, sending slivers into his face. Pawing at his eyes, Vent dropped flat and stared toward the bank, but couldn't see a thing through the blur. Removing his bandanna, he carefully cleaned his eyes, then looked again and saw Bright's hat sticking over the top of a stump. Taking aim he fired just below the hat band and watched the headpiece sail away, revealing the stick upon which it had sat.

"The oldest trick in the world," Vent said aloud and punched out his empties and fed new shells into the loading gate of the .44.

Then he waited. If Bright attempted to leave the cover of the stump, Vent would kill him. If he remained where he was, he was no closer to crossing the river than when he first reached it. On the far side was Louisiana. All Bright had to do to get there was to kill Vent. Vent grinned mirthlessly and waited.

As the day wore on, Vent remained behind the tree and watched Bright's stump fortress. It must be damned hot out there, Vent thought, knowing Bright had to be hurting for water. With the river twenty feet behind him, Vent figured he was suffering every time he looked toward the coolness of its waters.

It was three in the afternoon when Bright finally broke. One minute it was deathly quiet there on the bank of the river and the next Bright leaped from cover and crouching over his .45s, began firing first one and then the other. Vent heard the crack of the slugs hitting limbs around him and suddenly he too stood up, stepped into the clear, raised his .44 and taking careful aim, shot Bright through the chest.

The man screamed, stumbled backward and went to his knees, then slowly raised his right hand gun and fired again. The bullet went far wide of its target as Vent walked slowly across the field toward his victim. Bright triggered the left-hand gun and the hammer fell on an empty and he cursed. Lifting the right-hand gun, he pulled its trigger. Empty. Falling over on his side, then, he dropped the guns and began inching his body along toward the river. Vent stopped ten feet from him and watched. There was no expression on his face.

"Oh God," Bright mumbled. "Oh God . . . it hurts . . . it hurts," then he was sobbing and as Vent watched, he made a last effort and his outstretched right hand fell into the waters of the Sabine and he muttered, "Home. . . ," and died.

Vent punched out his empties and reloaded and then five men rode from the timber and Vent recognized Cap Stalls. One of the Barbed-T cowboys was leading Bright's horse.

Riding up to where Vent stood, Stalls pulled in, and gazing down at the dead man, said in some admiration, "He sure as hell tried, didn't he?"

"He tried," Vent agreed, and walking to Bright's blaze-face, stepped into the saddle and rode into the trees and Stalls and his men looked at each other and followed. When they reached the trail, they found Vent exchanging saddles.

"Where to now?" Stalls asked.

"I got an Appaloosa to pick up in Nacogdoches," Vent said, and mounted the sorrel and led the way back west.

When he rode into the livery, the stableman came out, looked at the horse and observed, "Feller must be a magician. He's turned that gray into a sorrel."

"Gray caught a slug," Vent said. "I'll either leave this one in trade or pay for the other one."

As Stalls and his men watched, the liveryman walked around the horse and made his inspection, opened its mouth to check its teeth, then examined each hoof, finally stepping back and staring at him for a long minute.

"What about the feller was riding this here horse?" the liveryman asked.

"He won't be needing him anymore," Vent said quietly.

The liveryman flashed Vent a glance and said, "Suits me. It's a deal."

Almost a month to the day that Vent rode out of Nacagdoches, he arrived at Lost Lake in the Colorado Rockies and found Owney Sharp sitting on the front porch, his feet up on the porch rail. A cup of coffee was on the bench beside him. Leaning on the saddle horn, Vent looked at his old friend and said, "You look coyote thin, neighbor."

"You look some gaunted up yourself," Sharp countered.

Then the door was flung open and a squealing bundle of femininity burst out and ran off the porch and Vent dismounted and she threw her arms around him and hugged him and gave him a resounding kiss and then leaned far back in his arms and looked at his face closely. "You look terrible, Vent Torrey. You put that horse up and come right in here and let me fix you something to eat."

Grinning, Vent said, "Yes, ma'am," and Sharp smiled

and observed, ''Your sister is a woman who cannot allow a man to get thin.''

''She got that from her maw,'' Vent said, and followed her inside, where he found his brother-in-law sitting at the table before a large plate of steak and potatoes. Looking up, he grinned. ''The prodigal son,'' he said, then raised his voice and called, ''Hey, Owney, chuck's on.''

Sitting down Vent suddenly felt a great weight pass from his shoulders as he looked around at his sister, her husband, and his old friend. The faces of Denton and Carroll Rose passed in review across his mind's eye, then they were replaced by Crimp Blair, Whitey Beard, old man Jordan, Dance Evers, Dan Stump, and Mick O'Reilly. The last face to appear was that of Canefield Bright. Shrugging then, Vent glanced at Sharp, who had been watching him. Sharp asked, ''Getting rid of old ghosts?''

''Something like that,'' Vent replied and relaxed. He was home again.

Watch for

DARK NEMESIS

next in the LEATHERHAND series
from Pinnacle Books

coming in September!

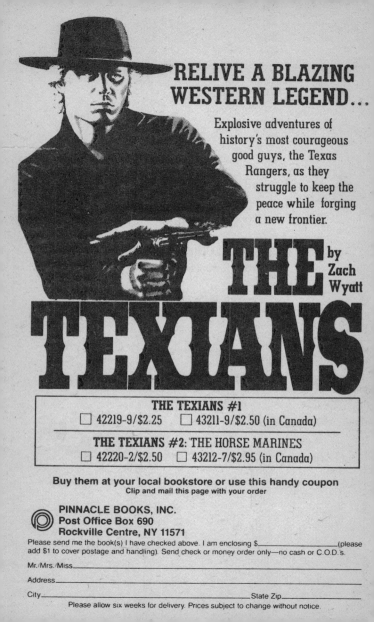